Dearest Kath[...]
                ma[...]
renewed he[...]
        may our great God bless you &
comfort you.

                        Love & Prayers,
                        Penny
                        Jeremiah 33:3

# Out of the Mouths of *Babes*

## J. LAURA CHANDLER

WESTBOW
PRESS®
A DIVISION OF THOMAS NELSON
& ZONDERVAN

WestBow Press books may be ordered through booksellers or by contacting:

WestBow Press
A Division of Thomas Nelson & Zondervan
1663 Liberty Drive
Bloomington, IN 47403
www.westbowpress.com
1 (866) 928-1240

ISBN: 978-1-5127-9590-5 (sc)
ISBN: 978-1-5127-9591-2 (hc)
ISBN: 978-1-5127-9589-9 (e)

Library of Congress Control Number: 2017911283

Print information available on the last page.

WestBow Press rev. date: 07/17/2017

# Dedication

*As Job so wisely speaks from the scripture, "My life passes more swiftly than a runner," and so* my *life...
In this last passage of my earthly journey, Jacob, Kenadee, Kace, Chloe and Wayne have given me love, joy and purpose. Their purity and innocence have revealed the many faces of God and enriched my life immeasurably. This novel is dedicated to them.*

# *Chapter 1*

## *2007*

As Al would reflect countless times, this past year had taken him to the highest highs and stranded him in the deepest valleys. He had been under fire from the evil one, yet he had also known and rested in the wings of angels. The gloss of wishful thinking had ended when Dana and his son, Cole, left for Montana two weeks earlier. His multimillion-dollar business was flourishing, but he was haunted by his admission in court the previous day that he had murdered the mother of a three-year-old boy and wife of a prominent attorney—a murder that took place some twenty years ago. Yes, it was self-defense, but his actions were responsible for killing another person! But quite beyond these burdens, his God was sovereign and caused everything to work together for the good of those who love him. *Oh, my mighty Savior and Redeemer, I abide in you and you in me, so I rest my case and ask you to sing over me tonight so that I may sleep deeply.*

The first signs of morning light were peeping through the top of the closed curtains in Al's bedroom. Even though he had a crippling caution about meeting with Richard James, head of his company—and a kind and brilliant guy—he wanted to sleep and dream again of his lovely Cindy and pure, angelic Molly. "I must be brave and not foolish or deluded about the realities this day will hold," he said to himself.

Then he closed his eyes and prayed silently. *God, please guide me in making a wise decision that will not further risk the company's good standing. The public may have a strong opinion of vengeance, which is understandable, so I am asking you to bestow great wisdom on Richard as he advises me of the next step regarding our business plans. The opposition may be fierce, and how I covet your intervention, Lord. Thank you, Father.*

Al had been in constant contact with Dana. Cole had become quite the photographer as he and Dana rode horses together in full view of the majestic mountains of her family's Montana ranch. With a bit of distance from the publicized event in St. Louis, Al savored the relief he felt regarding Cole being protected from knowledge of his involvement in a crime. He also recognized that this was a temporary reprieve, for in three more days, Dana and Cole would return, and the truth would then be revealed in its entirety.

"Yes, Lord, let me live in today without trepidations of what tomorrow will bring."

Al opened the drapes and beheld the beautiful morning. After making a pot of coffee, he took his first morning cup and sat in the little courtyard adjoining his bedroom. He and Cole had been living in their new home for only a short time. It was within walking distance of Cole's school, and the layout of their home was perfect for father and son. Cole's little pad was upstairs, and his was downstairs. Richard James had been responsible for the design and furnishings of this beautiful home. Al had consented to move from Kingston after Cindy and Molly were killed in an automobile accident. It was a weighty decision since St. Louis was the place his life of twenty years ago was one of drugs and crime. *Lord, certainly you can see how our poor choices and regrets continue to play havoc in our minds. Oh, that you would release the enemy's grasp. You fight our battles for us, and this is the day you have made. Thank you, my Father.*

As Al stirred around in the kitchen, the thoughts of Cole being home and the two of them preparing meals together warmed his heart. The sun rays shone throughout the kitchen and spilled into the great room. Al caught his breath as the warmth reminded him of that poignant moment in the courtroom when he felt that angels transported him to a place of glorious bliss and heavenly refuge. Even the judge had been taken aback by the brilliant light. He would never know if anyone else saw what he felt and the judge witnessed, but he was confident that God's truth and mercy had pierced the heart of the judge. After all, God changes the course of a river and the heart of a king, so why not the mind of a judge? "Yes, it shall be a great day, for you, oh Lord, are the mighty king and great warrior, and we shall reign victorious with you!"

———〰〜♒♒〜〰———

Richard had arrived early at the home office of Kingston's Best and was drinking his third cup of coffee while trying to digest the front page of the newspaper. There was a picture of Al Statham on the front steps of the courthouse with a group of reporters surrounding him.

Surprisingly, Al appeared to be totally composed. Richard and many of the key people in their company were still in a state of shock regarding Al's involvement in a crime twenty years ago. The achievements of their business started with meager beginnings, and it was obvious that everything Al touched had huge profits attached. The man exhibited integrity and humility and had a heart for the underdog, always.

He could remember how Al had always been adamant about giving those less fortunate a chance to better themselves. There were times Al would personally bring someone on board who had no chance of getting employment elsewhere. Surprisingly, most of these employees had not only bettered themselves but had also been major assets for the company. Al had spoken on occasion about being given second chances himself, and it was apparent he wanted to pass this forward.

There had been several acquisitions in the last year that had raised more profit for their company than Richard could believe. Daily, adjustments were being made for expansion and diversification. There was little time to get to know employees in top management because new people were being employed so rapidly. It seemed that everything Al touched was taken to unpredicted heights. How was this possible?

Al greeted Ms. Marks before entering Richard's office. He remembered that devastating day that Ms. Marks told him there was an urgent call for him. He excused himself from a meeting and took the call.

It was Pastor Anthony calling to say Cindy and Molly had been killed in an accident.

It now seemed like a lifetime ago that Al had lost his wife and daughter, but it was less than a year. So much had happened in such a short time.

*Dear Lord, knowledge and wisdom are miles apart, and today I need your divinely enabled application of truth. You possess all truth and are my ultimate source. I am relying on you to unfold your hidden treasures of wisdom. At all cost, keep me humble, dear Jesus, so I may serve you and not man.*

*Oh, Lord, I take great comfort in a passage of Nehemiah where you mentioned if we return and obey your commands and live by them, even if we are exiled, you will bring us back to a place where your name can be honored. Should I be an outcast, give me grace to totally trust and abide in you regardless of circumstances or shame.*

"Good morning, Al. Please make yourself comfortable while I order more coffee."

"None for me, Richard. I need a perfectly clear and sound mind this morning, for I'm quite sure we will be talking through many aspects of the business and my personal life as well."

"Yes, Al. I want to hear what you have to say before assessing anything to do with the company."

Al shared every piece of information about his personal life that he could remember. He went into detail about his involvement with drugs in his past life and how he had sold Kate Marshall cocaine. When he could no longer furnish her with the amount she wanted, she had tried to stab Al with a kitchen knife, only to inflict a fatal wound in her own side.

Kate had been mentally ill, and even though Al did not murder her, he felt responsible for her death. He told Richard about how his life had radically changed when he accepted Jesus as his Savior, and at that point, God had blessed his life abundantly. He shared many of the events that happened when he lived in Kingston with his wife, Cindy, and daughter, Molly, along with Cole.

He didn't forget to mention that sweet lady, Mayme, either. What a dear soul she was, and how her life played out before him spoke volumes about forgiveness and healing. Healing always comes with forgiveness. She was responsible for him coming to know the Lord. She gave him another chance when he was down on his luck. Yes, God transformed him and blessed him in a mighty way.

Al also shared how he believed God showed him favor with Judge Ray Lewis in the courtroom the previous day; otherwise, he would not be a free man today!

Richard sat mesmerized by Al's account of his life. Who would have guessed this man's experiences in his early life?

Richard knew that everything Al touched was prosperous, and at the same time, he felt that both Al and the company needed to be protected from public opinion in the St. Louis area, especially since this was the home office for their company. There was simply no way of knowing how all of the publicity would affect the health of the company. There had been such an increase in profits and mergers just in the last six months, and Richard knew much caution should be taken in safeguarding the reputation of Al.

After a long pause, Al broke the silence. "What are your thoughts, Richard?"

"First, I want protection for you and Cole, and then I want our company to be sheltered from negative publicity that would reduce the value of our stock and also run the risk of contracts being broken on present acquisitions."

"Certainly, I agree with you. You must know that I don't have the presence of mind right now to be objective, Richard. I'll have to rely on your suggestions and advice. In the past, you have made excellent choices and brought in profits for this company that are amazing. I do trust your judgment."

"Al, I want to meet with members of the board and our legal advisor this afternoon before moving forward on any changes. I know you have quite a bit to think about, and since you're expecting Cole's return, there are probably many things on the domestic front that need your attention. Why don't you take off the next couple of days, and we'll meet again the day after tomorrow. I will tell you this … I have a strong feeling that we need to relocate you and Cole for the next year or two, and there are some options I need to thoroughly check out in some of our offices abroad. I'll know more after talking with others in the company. Go home and get some much needed rest, Al."

Al smiled in his accepting and composed way. "You are right, of course. I need time to adjust to many things right now and pray for God's will and leading. I'll be in touch, Richard."

Dana noticed that Cole fell asleep just as the plane reached cruising speed. This child had been such a joy to her and her family. He was a natural with horses. Come to think of it, he was a natural with everything. Her family had fallen in love with this little cowboy, and Cole had a hard time saying goodbye to everyone upon departing. She had read the morning paper earlier. Al had been in touch by phone and shared the highlights of all the courtroom drama concerning his crime of twenty years ago. She was still in shock and wondered how this would affect her relationship with Al. She could not digest the fact that Cole's dad had been entangled in a murder and indirectly in a kidnapping, too!

*How could I have thought about a serious relationship with a man who was a criminal!*

Dana had a great job as a reporter and journalist. The article she wrote about Al's company a few months back had not only boosted profits for Kingston's Best but had directly been responsible for her recent promotion. She loved her work, and after growing up on a ranch in Montana with many hardships, she had no desire to leave St. Louis. Even the recent visit with Cole brought heartache, as she witnessed her parents and brothers having to work long hours to make ends meet, especially in the frigid winters. She needed to use good judgment and not be ruled by her heart regarding a relationship with Al. Poor Cole; he knew nothing about his dad's early life. This was going to be a shock to this little guy and further break his heart. His heart was still so tender from losing his mom and little sister, and Dana could tell that he put on a brave front for the sake of his dad. The little family had been through more than Dana could bear to think about.

---

Members of the board may not have been thoroughly convinced regarding Richard's suggestion to let Al continue to be a viable part of the company, but the idea of relocating him to England finally won the approval of all. Richard needed to do further research before talking to Al about this decision. It was indeed sad that Al's past had turned the hearts and minds of those who once held the utmost respect for him to stone cold. His recurring thought was that Al's past was about another person, not the man Richard had witnessed the past two years. "Amid this perplexing tangle, though, Al is an honorable man with a composure few possess," Richard whispered under his breath.

Before Richard could call it a day and leave the office, he jotted down several ideas that might work for Al. The Halifax office in England was one of the busiest and most profitable locations other than St. Louis. Leeds was only thirty minutes from Halifax, so Al could possibly keep a low profile in Leeds and on occasion meet with managers to share his opinion and still offer suggestions on quality control. "Yes, this just may appeal to Al, especially if a country place could be purchased, so Cole would have an opportunity to ride horses, which is fast becoming his passion!"

———~~vooevooevoovw———

Cole burst through the front door with Dana trailing slowly behind.

"Hey, Dad, I missed you more than you could have ever missed me, and I have so much to tell you and lots of pictures, too!"

Al swung Cole around and held him tight. This child was his life. "So, you have two weeks' worth of experiences and pictures to share?"

"Dana, please come in and make yourself at home. I'll get us all some refreshments."

"No, Al. I'm expected to be in the office early a.m., and it has been a long day. Really, I must go."

Al took her hand gently in his and held it for a moment. His sincere smile made her heart ache for what might have been. She could not place behind her the man that he was and only see him for the man that stood before her. How she longed for her mind to not play the negative record of his criminal past, but she could not help herself. Saying goodbye to Cole was the most difficult part. How she loved this young boy who was the very image of his dad. She must flee and try to forget!

"Dana, I don't have the words to express my appreciation for your taking Cole to visit your family in Montana. I'm sure this trip will always be the highlight of his young life. We do have a lot to work through, and I realize that you need to dedicate your time to your career now, so know our door is always open to you. I shall forever be grateful for God bringing you into our lives."

As Al opened the door for Dana to depart, Cole ran to her and clung in a tight hug. "Ms. Dana, I love you. Please come visit soon so we can ride horses together at the stables!"

———————

Richard had spent the two previous evenings at home on his computer researching an appropriate place for Al to relocate. Why he felt the need to personally handle it was a mystery, but he had found Al's present home, and he wanted to make sure that Al knew how valuable he was to the company. The country home he had made an offer on was on the outskirts of Leeds. The house had three levels, manicured grounds around the home, and seventy acres of meadowland with a small lake, plus an adjoining two hundred acres of woods. There were stables that were not in use and probably needed some repairs, but that could easily be done. There was a beautiful and stately stone fence that graced the meadow and provided a secure place to ride horses. The entire place looked as though it had been created just for Al and Cole. He could envision Al and Cole building a few bee colonies, gardening, and riding horses together. There were also open fields adjoining some of the property … plenty of places to roam and explore!

His meeting this morning with Al was scheduled for 8:30. Al's present house would bring a handsome profit, and if Al was not amenable to relocating, the country estate could easily turn a profit as well. With all the bases covered, Richard poured another cup of coffee and again reflected on the last few days' events concerning Alfred Statham's personal life.

Al nodded and smiled at Ms. Marks before entering Richard's office. "Good morning, Richard."

"Hey, Al, would you mind closing my door?"

Al shut the door and for the first time in quite a while felt somewhat anxious. *Lord, I thought those days were behind me. I know you go before me, so I'm trusting you to keep me in your will, dear Lord.*

"Al, it is always good to see you and a pleasure to be in your company. I know we have a few challenges right now, so I'm going to be as clear and factual as possible. After my meeting with the board, I decided that it would be best for you and our company to relocate you and Cole to

England for a season. This is not set in stone; certainly, you are not required to go unless you elect to do so. But I have taken the liberty of securing you a home in Leeds, which is about thirty minutes from our main office in Halifax. We are in need of someone like yourself who could monitor quality control in the Halifax office, and I cannot think of anyone more qualified than you. This office is expanding, so you will not be the only person relocating. I really think if you decide to move, you and Cole need at least a month's vacation after settling in before you feel obliged to make an appearance at the operations center. I'm sure Cole will have major adjustments leaving his friends here in St. Louis, but perhaps relocating to a place where he can enjoy horses will soften the blow. I cannot begin to imagine how difficult all this is for you, Al. I am so sorry."

"Thanks, Richard. When you offered to relocate us from Kingston to St. Louis, the physical move was totally seamless, and I know you will do everything in your power to orchestrate this move in a way that would lessen my stress. I have procrastinated about telling Cole anything about my past life. Actually, I've just been reveling in his presence since he returned from Montana. You know this child is in many ways a companion and comfort for me. Cole has the maturity level of an adult, and yet I see a tender and vulnerable spirit that compels me to keep my guard up regarding protecting him. There is not a day that passes that I don't witness his profound loneliness and grief for his mother, and I still have such a hollowness in my heart to the extent I feel ill-quipped to give Cole the balance he needs and deserves in life."

"Al, do you see that Cole's love of horses could be the very thing that he could plug into with your encouragement and participation?"

"I probably see less clearly right now than I have in quite a while. Honestly, I'm thankful you pointed this out. I need objective direction, Richard. I trust your judgment, and I respect you as a friend. Seems you've been through mega challenges with regard to my personal life. Is it really fair for the company to keep bailing me out?"

"Al, you *are* the company. If it were not for your meager beginnings in the bee business, we would have no business, not to mention your wise input in hiring the right people with a heart to grow our company. You instinctively target the right qualities in people. You see attributes of integrity and commitment in people that our personnel staff does not see.

Some of the employees you have personally been responsible for hiring have proved to increase our profits in an unbelievably short time. It is a privilege to be a small part of helping you and Cole through this difficult passage right now. It is my desire to ease your pain, Al."

"I want to talk with Cole first. I need to tell him everything about my past life before we embark upon moving again. Give me three days to get back with you, okay?"

"You got it!"

———

Al took his first cup of coffee with him upstairs to awaken Cole. He did not want another day to pass without his son knowing the truth about everything. Cole had given his heart to Jesus, and Al knew God could get them through this challenge together. Both had spoken on many occasions about their total dependence upon the Lord.

"Good morning, little man. Time to rise and shine!"

"Oh, Dad, it seems too early. Whose turn is it to fix breakfast?"

"We'll do it together. You make up the pancake batter, and I'll flip the pancakes and fry bacon. Is that a deal?"

"Hey, Dad, I'll race you to the kitchen!"

The sun shone so brightly through the bay windows and cast dancing shadows of the birds singing in the trees. Already there were wonderful memories to reflect upon since they had moved into this lovely home. Al wanted to move forward with God, and that meant always making major adjustments. He reminded himself that "faith" is also a verb, which always requires action. *Lord, help me to share all the truth with Cole. I ask only that your Holy Spirit help him to receive this information in a way that his heart will not be hurt beyond his present pain and profound grief. Thank you, my Father.*

"Cole, let's skip the dishes for now. Come sit by me on the sofa; I need to talk with you, son."

"Sure, Dad. Are you okay? You sound a little serious. What's up?"

"Son, what I'm about to share with you is going to be both surprising and disappointing; actually shocking would be a better word."

"Dad, you can tell me anything. You know I'll understand."

"I'm going to tell you about my past life before I met and married your mom and before you were born. Actually, this is all about my poor choices, mistakes, consequences, and regrets—all of which can be summed up as sins."

"Dad, we all sin, but when we ask for forgiveness and turn from our sins, God is faithful to forgive us."

"You are correct, son, and I know God has forgiven me, but due to some of the consequences of my sins, there are certain things I must tell you, so we both can move on in God's will. If possible, try to hear me out while I have the courage to speak of my past, and then I'll answer any and all questions. Okay?"

Al tried his best to speak on Cole's level of understanding and share every shameful and painful aspect of his past life. He was emotional and tearful most of the time, and Cole appeared to be shocked and uneasy.

"Cole, are you okay?"

"You don't have to go to jail—right, Dad?"

"All charges were dropped, son, and I am a free man, but there may still be some consequences we must work through. One big decision that you and I have to make is regarding where we live. At least for a short period of time, I do not need to remain in St. Louis because of negative publicity impacting our personal lives and perhaps the reputation of our company."

"Oh, Dad, what about Ms. Dana?"

"We will pray about all of this, and the Lord will go before us. You know He has the Master plan. Mr. James has recommended that we relocate to England. That would mean a new home, new school, saying goodbye to friends here, and allowing the Lord to help us discover a new life in another country. I've overloaded you with things to think about, haven't I, son?"

"Will we see Ms. Dana?"

"I cannot say. That would be left up to her, Cole. I know the two of you have so much common ground regarding horses, and I know you enjoy her company. I think the world of Ms. Dana, too, and I'm hopeful that she'll continue to be a part of our lives. Should we move to England, there is plenty of land for us to own horses. There are even stables on the grounds where our home would be located. You would be able to ride anytime you wanted. Quite honestly, I'm looking forward to riding with you. Do you think you can teach me how to ride?"

"Of course. You'll be a natural, Dad!"

"Do you have any questions right now, Cole, about my past?"

"Maybe one. What happened to the little boy of the mother who killed herself?"

"That's a good question. The short answer is even though he was kidnapped, he was later reunited with his dad. And the long answer, we'll save for another time, if that is okay with you."

"Okay, Dad. Guess I need to help you with the dishes, and we'll start packing!"

"Oh my, you sound like your mother now ... living in the moment with much joy!"

Cole fell on his dad's chest in sobs. "Oh, Dad, I miss her so much." Al's heart felt the same, and he knew that Cole tried to remain strong for his sake. All of the seriousness of Al sharing his past had taken his boy by surprise, and he knew both of them needed stability in their lives. Perhaps they would remain in England for more than just a season. *Lord, you know what we need. I know what we have waiting for us in heaven is extraordinary and more than we could imagine, and all the pain of this life will pale in significance, but, dear Jesus, help me to make wise choices for my precious son. Choices that will build his confidence in you, dear Lord.*

"Cole, everything is okay, even in our pain, uncertainty of life, and the profound grief we have for your mom. We know God comforts, heals, restores, and fights our battles. Son, our hearts will mend because our Lord is faithful. I'm confident we're going to make many friends when we move to England, and we're also going to find a church where we will be connected to the community and serve the Lord. Who knows—you may decide to sing in the choir again! Your mom would want us to look to the Lord for our joy and strength and go forward. Don't you think?"

"You are right, Dad. Guess I just needed a good cry."

"It is always okay to cry. We never need to apologize about our sadness over anything. In a way, God uses our tears to cleanse the soul. We're going to be just fine. Today is a new day with new mercies, and we have an exciting life to embrace with wonderful surprises ahead!"

———~ɯɯ෧ଦୟୖଓଡ଼ଡ଼ଡ଼ଡ଼ଡ଼ɯ———

Dana could not seem to concentrate, and all motivation regarding her promotion had come to a halt. She was totally unprepared for the crisis she was going through with her heart. Al and Cole lived a faith that she was not acquainted with in the least. Both of them seemed equipped to sail through extremely hard times because of their strong faith. She longed to just sit and talk with them as she had in the past. Both had a confidence that she had not witnessed in others. It was as though she were in life's ultimate storm, and all shelters were failing her, crumbling under her feet. Where was her confidence? She had been in such a fog the last few days with utterly no direction in business or her personal life. She was discovering that her feelings for Al went much deeper than she could have imagined. Her heart had become insensitive when she found out about Al's past. She certainly had not demonstrated brotherly love, and she knew if things had been reversed, Al would support and embrace her with loving kindness. She felt such shame regarding her thoughts and coldness. Perhaps cold was a little harsh, but certainly she had been cool, especially the evening she took Cole home. Al was the same; only she had changed, and she had made it abundantly clear to him that she did not desire even the touch of his hand on hers. She must not play the record of regret. Time would take care of everything.

"Dana, Mr. Davidson wants you to come to his office at your earliest convenience."

"Thanks, Vera. Please tell him I'll be there in five."

Dana was happy to have Vera as an assistant. She was a sincere young lady and oddly enough possessed some of the sweetness she had witnessed in Cole. This was their first week together as a team, but in some ways, Dana felt she had known Vera much longer.

"Vera, I will probably only be a few minutes in Mr. Davidson's office, and when I return, we need to get organized, and I would like for you to schedule a couple of appointments for me."

"Sounds great. I'll be waiting!"

———～∿～◦◟◦◝◟◦◝◦∿～———

*Father, I thank you that you did not leave me with condemnation, judgment, and hopelessness but a renewal through your Holy Spirit and justification through the precious and powerful blood of Jesus Christ! If you were not watching over me and guarding me, all of these challenges set before me would only be obstacles, but I know that you are in control, so I take great comfort in relying totally on you.*

Al had been waiting to see Richard to let him know that he and Cole would be willing to relocate, but before leaving the country, he felt strongly about trying to get an appointment with Judge Ray Lewis. In addition to making sure he was a free man, he wanted to ask the judge what he had seen in the courtroom that day that had persuaded him to drop all charges. Al could have read things secondhand in the paper, but for some reason, he had tossed his daily newspapers in the trash.

As he watched Ms. Marks, he could not help but notice her gracious nature in handling Richard's phone calls. She had a radiant glow about her, and Al knew in his spirit she was a kind and loving person and one who knew the Lord. She smiled in a way that he knew she did not judge him. *Thank you, Lord, for this helps me to better accept myself.*

"Mr. Statham, Mr. James can see you now."

"Thank you, Ms. Marks. You've been very kind."

She nodded and smiled and escorted him to Richard's office.

"I hope I'll be receiving good news from you this morning, Al! I admit I've had my reservations about moving ahead so quickly and hope I have not appeared headstrong in this new direction to relocate you."

"Not at all, Richard. Your offer is generous and seemingly well thought out. You have a gift for being decisive and yet thorough. I do believe you weighed all the facts in an objective way for the company as well as my personal life. Cole took all the news like the trooper he has always been. Not sure why I had so many trepidations about telling him. Losing his mom and sister, plus suddenly being plunged into my awful past has pitched him into a posture of adulthood. I pray that I can give him back part of his childhood that has been stripped from him. Having a month off to think of only my son's needs and be in the moment with him is what I dare to dream right now. It is the one thought that keeps me going forward in a positive mode."

"Al, you have a great attitude, and I admire your courage and wisdom."

"Richard, there is one thing that I need to resolve before embarking to leave and go to another country."

"I'm listening, Al."

"I really need to make sure that I am legally allowed to leave the state of Missouri as well as the United States."

"Already covered that, Al. You are in no way legally bound for further investigation. Our attorney has all the documentation on your case, and you are a free man. Actually, that was the first thing we looked into before I met with the members of the board regarding relocating you."

"You are such an asset, Richard. We are all privileged to have you running our company!"

"We're a team, Al, and you, my friend, are one of the most vital members!"

"This is moving quite fast, and I guess if I inquired about airline tickets for Cole and me, you would hand them to me, right?"

"Exactly!"

---

Dana was in another zone since meeting with Mr. Davidson. He gave her the assignment of interviewing Al Statham. When she initially interviewed Al and wrote an article in the *Entrepreneur* magazine, plus a column in the paper, about the meager beginnings of Kingston's Best, the publicity set off fireworks. She had gotten her promotion at *Entrepreneur* because of that one story. Al's company had been flooded with even more profits, and in many ways he had become a hero. It seemed he was living the American dream.

She could not imagine intruding on Al's privacy, nor could she think about the personal pain an interview would inflict on both of them. She had told Mr. Davidson she would think about requesting an audience with Mr. Statham, but she had many reservations at this time. He mentioned that she needed to be the person to do a follow-up interview since she had originally interviewed Al and his son. She at least needed the courage to do some research and know where the public's posture was regarding Al and his company, but she felt pressured, alone, and drifting with no clear direction.

She and Vera had their work cut out for them. She had seen the publicity in the newspapers dwindle the last couple of days, but there were, of course, monthly magazines that would splash Al's face on front covers to capitalize on the sale of their merchandise. Money stops at nothing. More than anything, she wanted to build a case for Al, not against him, and that would take time because he was the most private person she knew. She now knew his past had much to do with the modest image he projected.

⸻ ·~•◦◦✿◦◦•~· ⸻

Cole was waiting for his dad to come home from the office as he gazed at all the beautiful fish in his bedroom aquarium. How he loved this house, his friends, and Ms. Dana. He had just begun to enjoy his new life after losing his mom and sister. When he thought of his dad being mixed up and getting into trouble when he was younger, Cole broke out in a cold sweat and wanted to throw up. He did not want his dad to think he was disappointed in him, so he kept much to himself.

"Hey, Cole! I'm home, son! Come on down and let's go get a foot-long at the little hot dog stand downtown. When I started home, the craving hit me for pickled relish, mustard, cheese, and onions atop a foot-long, but I needed you to be with me so I could really enjoy it. Are you up for it?"

Placing all sadness behind, Cole ran down the stairs and said, "Sure thing, Dad. Let's do it!"

"Okay, jump in the car, and we'll be on our way. I have so much to tell you."

During their ride into the city, Al shared most of the things he and Richard had talked about. Cole's spirits lifted when his dad said he was going to have the next six weeks off from work, and they could be together getting settled in their new place and exploring the countryside in England.

They could smell the hot dogs a half block from the vendor's stand. There was no line, as the lunch rush had not yet begun. Each ordered a foot-long with a Coke and sat down on a bench nearby to enjoy munching and watching the people stroll by.

The weather was mild with a warm breeze, and Al's heart felt light. It seemed some of the pressure and heaviness of his whole life was beginning to lift. *Oh, Lord in heaven, could this be a new journey that you alone have prepared for me and my son? My Savior and Redeemer, you know I want nothing more than your will, and as you guide me, give me your peace, which the world cannot give. I want to laugh with Cole and experience some lighthearted moments, so let it be, dear Jesus.*

As Al deposited the trash in a container beside the vendor's corner spot, he looked up and made eye contact with Judge Lewis. He could never forget those intense blue eyes!

"Mr. Statham, I did not expect to see you this soon again."

"Hello, Your Honor."

"Who is this young fellow you have with you?"

"Judge Lewis, this is my son, Cole."

Cole extended his hand. "It is nice to meet you, sir."

"Well, it is indeed a pleasure to meet you."

"Judge, I believe it was meant for us to make contact today. I've wanted to speak with you about a decision my company has made for Cole and me. We are to relocate to England, and I did not feel comfortable leaving St. Louis without your knowing where we would be."

"I can believe that you would be concerned about such, for I believe you to be an honorable man and one who God has His hand on. Cole, you should be very proud of your dad. He came forth to save another's life."

"Judge, I do have one question to ask before we depart. What did you actually see in the courtroom to give you the confidence to set me free?"

"Al, you were surrounded by angels, and the light was so bright it was blinding. I know others did not see what I saw, but I would imagine you felt it."

"Yes, Your Honor. I will never forget being carried forward with no effort on my part and the comfort of our Lord's supernatural touch."

"You and your son go now and start a new life. May God bless you."

"May God bless you as well, Judge Lewis."

"Cole, seeing Judge Lewis again and being able to speak honestly to him has given me the green light regarding going to England. Mr. James has given me our airline tickets, and we're scheduled to leave America next week! Hope that is not too soon for you."

"Well, there is just one thing, Dad. Are we going to be able to see Ms. Dana and tell her goodbye?"

"Of course, son. Matter of fact, we'll give her a call when we return home this afternoon."

"Maybe she could come over tonight. We could make our famous fruit pie this afternoon when we get home."

"Sounds like a plan!"

"Oh, Dad, there is one more thing I would like to know, if you don't mind my asking."

"Sure, Cole."

"What did the judge mean by your coming forth to save another?"

"The short version is someone else was blamed for taking the life of Kate Marshall. I discovered it in the newspaper and immediately knew I had to come forward and tell the whole truth about everything, even if it meant my going to jail and not knowing what would become of you."

"That must have been the hardest thing you ever did, Dad!"

"Indeed. But God had prepared me with many trials prior to the courtroom trial, and I'm sure the death of your mom and Molly had plenty to do with refining my heart and life. Does that clear up a few things for the moment?"

"It does. Now let's go bake our fruit pie!"

The two rode home in silence. Al was reflecting on Dana being cool toward him when she and Cole returned from Montana. He did not want to impose on her—or anyone for that matter. But Cole would be so disappointed if he did not get to say goodbye to Dana before they went abroad. Yes, he would give her a call.

As he turned the key to the front entrance of the house, Al heard the phone ringing. Cole sprinted to the kitchen to answer it.

"It's for you, Dad!"

"Hello, this is Al Statham. May I help you?"

"Mr. Statham, I work with Ms. Fulton as her assistant, and she has the assignment of interviewing you and wanted me to check with you on a convenient time, if indeed you were open to being interviewed."

"Funny you should call at this particular time, because my son and I were going to call this afternoon and ask her to drop by for a visit!"

"Then you are consenting to be interviewed?"

"Tell Ms. Fulton my son and I are open to any of her questions."

"What time shall I tell Ms. Fulton to arrive?"

"Anytime after the next couple of hours."

"I shall. Thank you, Mr. Statham. Goodbye."

"Good day."

"Well, Cole, you have your wish. Ms. Dana will be visiting us later this afternoon. Let's get that pie baked!"

———⁓∘⊙⊙⊙∘⁓———

As Dana neared Al's neighborhood, she wondered why she was beset with fear. It was more than just being anxious about the interview. Was she a prisoner of her own fears? How could she relax and conduct herself as she always had with Al and Cole? More than anything, how could she judge Al so harshly for things that happened so long ago? He had never lied to her or betrayed her in any way. He had been totally honest in the short time they had been acquainted. A friendship actually defined their relationship, so why was she being so critical and fearful?

As she got out of her car, Cole ran out to greet her with hugs. "Oh, Ms. Dana, it is so good to see you!"

"I'm glad to see you, too!"

"I have missed riding horses together, but we will be buying horses of our own soon!"

"Really?"

"We have so much to tell you. Please come in. Dad and I also baked a pie this afternoon for you."

"Oh, Cole, you and your dad are so thoughtful."

Al stood at the front entrance, composed as always, with that natural smile of his. Cole was a carbon copy of his handsome dad.

"Hello, Dana. We are so happy to have you visit us. Come in and enjoy a warm slice of pie and a cup of hot tea."

"I would love to. How well I remember your famous fruit pie. Actually, you introduced me to it the very first time we met."

"You and Cole have a seat on the couch, and I'll bring our refreshments over from the kitchen. I would imagine you two have a lot of catching up to do!"

"Hey, Dad, may I tell Ms. Dana about our place in England?"

"Sure, go ahead."

Dana's heart sank. What kind of news would she be hearing?

"Ms. Dana, Dad knows all the facts. I just have a few, but I'll share what I know. We are leaving St. Louis next week and moving to Leeds, England. Our house and stables are waiting on us but no horses yet. We'll have to get busy looking for a few gentle horses, and we have a whole month to work together on our options until Dad has to go back to work! Isn't that great news?"

"Well, I hardly know what to say. I'm rather caught off guard, but it sounds exciting for the two of you!"

"All right, service with a smile, you two."

"Oh man, Dad, this is your best pie yet!"

"Maybe you've been off your feed for a while, son!"

"Al, this is really great. I remember that this was your older friend's recipe. The lady you told me about who helped you redirect your life?"

"Yes, Mayme was her name. Bless her sweet heart. She and God brought about miraculous changes in my heart and my lifestyle. Seems like a lifetime ago, too. I'd like to remember Ms. Mayme as God's angel with a personal mission."

"Ms. Dana, would you and Dad excuse me? I know the two of you want to catch up, and I have packing upstairs I need to stay focused on. Would you mind?"

"Not at all, Cole. You are such a thoughtful young man, and I adore you."

"Same here, Ms. Dana. I'll be back down before you leave."

"Al, I'm shocked to learn of your move! Was this a decision of yours or your company?"

"Sounds like your interview has started. Don't you want to turn on your recorder?"

"Not this time, Al. And I cannot say if I will write an article on your misfortune of late or not."

"Dana, there was so much good that came out of my stepping up to tell the truth about my past. So I really cannot view anything that was revealed as a misfortune. I'm confident God allowed everything to happen so His purpose could be fulfilled in many people's lives."

"Al, this is just me personally wanting to know how you feel and view things, not anything for the public to hear from an interview. Do you think God took your wife and daughter from you because of your past actions?"

"I cannot say that I have not had perhaps a passing thought as thus, but the Bible tells us that we are forgiven when we repent, and God remembers our sins no more. Our sins do carry a price, and many times there can be lingering consequences, but our great God causes all things to work together for good for those who love Him, and I love Him with all my heart."

"There will always be people who think you should have been punished for your past. What do you think about that?"

"When I decided to tell of my past in court to Judge Lewis, I was prepared to face the consequences, which could obviously include loss of my freedom, loss of Cole, and I don't know what else, but Judge Lewis thought otherwise."

"Do you think your business will suffer because of this?"

"I pray that it does not affect the income of those trying to provide a living for their families."

"Is your move to England a decision made by your company?"

"It is but certainly done with much thought. Let's say it was an option for me to consider, and after hearing Mr. James share his thoughts, I felt it would be a good move for Cole and me at this time. It could be a permanent move or only for a season. Right now I'm taking one step at a time and one day at a time."

"Al, I am still stunned over this decision to move to another country!"

"I've not given it much thought. We have such little time to get things packed, so the details are a blessing, I suppose. Mr. James has purchased a country place with acreage for us, so we'll be able to buy a few horses and enjoy riding. You'll have to come visit us once we get settled. We'll send you an airline ticket whenever you have some more time off. I know Cole would be so excited about the prospects of your visiting us in England!"

"That's a kind and sweet gesture, Al. I truly wish you and Cole the very best on your new journey. St. Louis has been a great location for my profession thus far, so I plan to buckle down and see where my career takes me here. I do have to admit I have a lack of motivation at the moment and need to work on taking a more positive approach to getting back on track."

"Dana, I know that the things you are viewing in my life right now probably place a negative twist on your outlook, but please know that our great God has the plan. Just lay your burdens down and look to Jesus for His peace. After all, we have a sovereign God. Yes, we have a few choices but little control in our lives."

"Al, you make it sound so easy. When I was younger and living in Montana, we all worked together with purpose. My family was united for the greater good of one another, and from what your life displays, you and Cole have that sense of harmony and unity with everyone you encounter. I just don't feel that connection right now."

"You will, Dana. Right now you are vastly disappointed over the facts of my past life, and perhaps your view of others needs to be more realistic. We do live in a fallen world and need never place anyone on a pedestal, for then we set ourselves up for disappointment. I am sorry that you see me in an unbecoming light right now, and I assure you, I understand. Try to see the present circumstances from a heavenly perspective, though. God is refining me and perhaps teaching you some valuable lessons as you look on. Cole and I will rise above this valley through God's mercy and grace. For me, the best thing about it all is a sense of sheer liberation regarding my past. The truth has been revealed, and I have been freed from guilt, condemnation, and fear. Yes, there may always be consequences, but in my heart of hearts, I'll know God has delivered me and better yet redeemed me!"

"Oh, Al, you make it sound so simple."

"It is simple, Dana. Jesus is the answer to everything we encounter and embrace in this life."

"Al, I do believe in a higher power, but I'm not at all sure about your Jesus!"

"When you want to talk further, we'll read some scripture together, Dana. I'm here for you, and when we move to England, I'll only be a phone call away. I'm sure our living in different countries will take us on separate paths, but I will always be grateful for your kindness in helping me with

Cole. You have been a Godsend, Dana. Cole and I will always keep you in our prayers and never forget you."

With tears running down her cheeks, Dana reached for Al's hand and held it tightly. "I'm sorry, Al. I wish I could move on easily like you do, but I cannot."

"There is no need to apologize. Why don't you run upstairs and say goodbye to Cole before you leave."

# Chapter 2

The days flew by, and before Al could digest the fact they were moving, he and Cole had boarded a jumbo jet, flown into Heathrow Airport in London, and were now on the last leg of their trip to their new home in Leeds. Their flight attendant was a kind young woman and had spent much of her time catering to an older woman across the aisle who seemed to have some health issues. Al had introduced himself to the elderly woman and mentioned that if she needed anything to let him know. The flight attendant introduced herself as Miss Joseph to the first-class passengers and mentioned that since the flight was short, no snacks would be served, but certainly beverages were available upon request. She had dimmed the cabin lights and stated arrival in Leeds was going to be around 6:00 a.m. London time.

Perhaps a quick nap would prepare him for the long day that was ahead. Richard had arranged for one of the company employees to meet the two of them and drive them to their country place. Apparently, this individual would help get them acclimated to their new home and community. It seemed only yesterday that he and Cole were getting settled in St. Louis! Change is inevitable, and it is always best not to have personal preferences or speculate about the future. All was in God's glorious hands, and many times over, he had witnessed thus, but still so many things were whirling around in his head.

Cole nudged his dad. "Have you thought any more about the dream I had about the plane crash, Dad?"

"I was just thinking about that, son."

"I know we'll be okay, even if our plane does crash. To be absent from the body is to be present with our Lord, Dad, so not to worry, right?"

"That is what our scriptures say, and there are no greater truths than what the Bible reveals to us."

"Dad, I want you to know that you are the best person I've ever known, and you've taught me so much about life here on earth as well as our eternal life with Jesus. You know how Ms. Dana mentioned that you and I have a great respect for one another?"

"Yes, I seem to remember."

"I believe Jesus places a holy respect in us toward others when we totally trust Him. I love and respect you above all others, except Christ! And, Dad, you know I love you with all my heart."

Al was so moved by his son's heartfelt expressions he could not help but cry. After reaching in his pocket for his handkerchief, Al covered his face and silently wept.

"Hey, Dad, it's going to be okay. I promise!"

"Cole, we have plenty of great times ahead. Now, you rest your heart, son. Jesus and I have your back!"

Cole immediately dropped off to sleep. His young face was absolutely angelic with such a pure, radiant glow. Al loved this child more than life, and time was speeding ahead so very quickly. He felt a deep desire to get out of the corporate world and concentrate on his son, his only son, his only family. *Oh, God in heaven, how thankful I am that you gave your only son up so I could have life, a most abundant life with my precious son. You saw me in all my wretchedness and loved me beyond myself. I continue to covet your will, and whatever that looks like, I'm in for the long haul. Cole and I are yours, heavenly Father. Please guard us on this flight and help us to start a new journey, a better life that can be more fully lived for you!*

Al had drifted off to sleep when he felt Cole tugging at his arm. "Dad, I smell something burning."

Miss Joseph alerted the first-class passengers that there seemed to be some mechanical problems, and for precaution, all oxygen masks were to be strapped on immediately.

In a muffled voice, Captain Conner announced that the control tower at Leeds had been notified that emergency clearance was needed. "We are fifty miles out from the airport, folks, so it won't be long before we land. The cockpit is experiencing smoke, so we're hoping to safely land where emergency personnel will be positioned to expedite the exit of all passengers. Carefully listen to the instructions of your flight attendant so departure from the plane can be done in an orderly fashion. We have your safety utmost in mind."

The elderly lady, Ms. Harold, across the aisle from Al, was gasping for breath. Al unbuckled his seat belt and went to her aid. Miss Joseph was checking all of the emergency equipment to ensure a fast exit. The captain had again spoken to notify everyone to remain calm. Cole noticed that one of the engines was on fire. He could see the runway lights clearly and prayed hard for the safety of everyone on board. There was a low murmur of voices over the entire plane, and he could hear some folks calling out to God for help. Al returned to his seat and buckled his seat belt after getting Ms. Harold as settled as possible. She was still struggling to breathe.

"Cole, you listen to everything Miss Joseph instructs you to do. I am going to assist Ms. Harold in any way possible to help her safely exit the plane. If I'm not able to get off the plane at the time you exit, just pray and know I'll be okay. More than anything, remain in God's confidence, and He'll carry us through this. Okay, son?"

"I'm not afraid, Dad. I know everything is going to be fine. God is our real captain."

As Captain Conner braced everyone for the emergency landing, Cole noticed that the flames of the engine were licking the entire wing on his side of the plane. The landing was unbelievably smooth, and the plane came to an abrupt halt. Miss Joseph grabbed Cole's hand and pulled him to the beginning of the line of passengers to exit. Al stayed behind trying to assist Ms. Harold. The crew opened the cockpit door to exit, and smoke quickly filled the first-class cabin.

Cole was on the ground and being carried along with the crowd to move away from the plane as quickly as possible. He kept looking back to see if his dad was safe but saw no sign of him. He could now see that the plane was on fire but could not make out any details because of the distance that separated him from the aircraft. *God, help my dad to make it to safety, in the Name of Jesus. Amen.*

The passengers were in shock as they watched the plane explode into flames. For as far and high as one could see, there were flames, and the heat could be felt from a great distance.

All passengers were being taken to the terminal. Cole knew no one and continued to pray that his dad would soon be with him. Suddenly, he felt a hand on his. Miss Joseph pulled him close to her. *Thank you, Lord, for this kind lady ... she is such a comfort to me. Oh, God, please let my dad be okay. Please, Father.*

Al and Captain Conner had escaped at last with Ms. Harold. They had placed her safely in an ambulance and then made sure everyone was positioned a safe distance from the burning aircraft. Both men had narrowly escaped, and as they walked shoulder to shoulder toward the terminal, there seemed to be a profound bond between the two of them.

"Captain Conner, my name is Al Statham."

"Stranger, you seem more like a brother now. If you had not been there to expedite Ms. Harold's exit from the plane, she and I would have been toast!"

"I am so grateful for this fresh breath of life. This early morning mist and fresh oxygen is bringing me back to life. How about you?"

"I must admit the smoke in the cockpit had just about overpowered us even with goggles and oxygen. Words cannot express how thankful I am to have survived. This is my first plane to lose, but I count it a gain since no lives were lost."

"Captain, I have been counting my blessings. God has protected all of us, and I am indeed thankful this morning to see anew His marvelous mercies!"

"Al, I could not agree more. By the way, are you vacationing or traveling on business?"

"You could say both. My son, Cole, and I are actually moving here from America. We've not yet seen our home and know very little about the area. Business brings us here, but I intend to show my son the countryside on horseback."

"Well, Al, you are talking to an old ranch hand. It would be my pleasure to show you and Cole around on horseback. There are some spectacular sights to view in Leeds, and viewing them from the back of a pleasure-riding horse is as good as it gets!"

"You sound like a rancher, not a pilot!"

"Pilot first but rancher at heart."

As both men approached the terminal, they could see a large crowd, so Captain Conner suggested they enter an alternate way to escape questions from the news media. This was a huge relief to Al, since all he could think of was finding his son.

"Al, the media is rarely kind to the airline industry when reporting a crash or tragedy. For some reason, the actual facts are processed through the media's fantasy machine and served on a tarnished platter stripped of the truth and laced with shock and awe."

"Captain Conner, we must be vigilant about positioning ourselves in God's truths or the world will keep us focused on the storms of this life rather than the goodness of God."

"I know you are right, but the glittering image of this world hunts me down daily like a pack of wolves, and I seem to be only reacting with raw human emotion."

"You may be embarking upon a new journey, Captain Conner!"

"Well, my friend, when you and your son get settled in your new place, I want an invitation to visit you and get to know you both!"

"And you shall. That's a promise."

All of the passengers had been escorted to a large private area, and those who needed medical attention were being checked out by several physicians and nurses. Also, phones, computers, and refreshments were provided for everyone. There were ample airline personnel, and what could have been utter chaos was surprisingly well organized. Miss Joseph continued to stay beside Cole. She would remain with him until his dad arrived.

"Cole, I am amazed how calm you've been throughout this entire ordeal. What a mature young man you are for your age."

"I think you've been amazingly calm, too. You took care of so many people and got them safely off the plane. I am impressed and so grateful!"

"Oh my, you talk like an adult. Just how old are you?"

"I am thirteen."

Walking up behind Cole, Al grabbed his son, held him tightly and told him how much he loved him.

"Oh, Dad, I'm so relieved to see you. I knew God would take care of us both, and you know what?"

"What's that, son?"

"We have a new friend already. Miss Joseph has taken the very best care of me!"

"Miss Joseph, we are indebted."

"Please call me India."

"Certainly, and you may call me Al."

"Al, there are a few documents that you'll need to sign off on so our airline can reimburse you for your loses. It may take awhile, so please make yourself as comfortable as possible and let me know if you or Cole need anything."

"India, we'll be fine, but there is one thing you might help us with. A gentleman from our company by the name of Nick Holland was supposed to meet us and escort us to our home, and I'm not sure how I should locate him here at the airport."

"Leave that to me, please. I'll make sure Mr. Holland is located and escorted to this lounge."

"Thanks, India."

Al could see the reporters gathering with their cameras. It seemed his life was destined to be in the public's view. *Dear Lord, you know my wishes are to have a simpler life and at least for a while keep a low profile, but how is this possible, and is this your will? Please, Father, let our lives and circumstances bring meaning to your kingdom purpose. We are your surrendered vessels.*

"Sir, I am a reporter from the *British Daily News*. I've been talking with Captain Conner, and he said without your help, his life and the life of a passenger could not have been spared. Could you tell us what you witnessed prior to departing the aircraft?"

"I would have to say Captain Conner handled every detail properly and professionally regarding the safety of all passengers. He is a perfect example of who I would want to pilot future flights for my son and myself."

"I'm told that Ms. Harold is indebted to both you and Captain Conner. I have a report that she is resting comfortably at one of our local hospitals and should be discharged after twenty-four-hour observation. I believe this was her first flight, and apparently she had trepidations about flying at her age. Her daughter lives here, and she will be taking care of her mom, so it seems all is well."

"That is indeed wonderful news. Sorry, I did not get your name."

"I am Nathaniel Germany. Please call me Nat. Mr. Statham, we are aware that your company, Kingston's Best, is relocating you to England, and we are so happy to welcome you!"

"Nat, thank you. We feel blessed to have arrived safely and are looking forward to getting settled in our home in Leeds and connecting with this community. Everyone has been most hospitable."

"Mr. Statham, I know you would like to relax with your son, so I will not hold you up any longer but do ask that you would give me an opportunity to interview you and your son after you have settled in our community."

"Sounds great."

India tapped Al on the shoulder. "I've located someone you'll be glad to see!"

"Mr. Statham, I am Nick Holland, and I am totally committed to taking care of you and your son and taking you to your new home. I have given Ms. Joseph all the information that is needed for the loss of your personal items, so we can be on our way, if you are ready?"

"Nice to meet you, Nick. We are more than ready to get home."

Cole had fallen asleep on one of the couches and looked so peaceful. *Thank you, Father, for your faithfulness. And so our new journey, our new life has begun and is already an open book! Thy will be done.*

The ride home was refreshing with beautiful hues from the early sun cascading across the countryside. Al had forgotten how much he missed the smells and sights of country living. He was so tired from the night's travel and challenges and at the same time excited to see their new home. He knew Cole would be hungry when he awoke because he could hear the little fellow's stomach growling. Cole had hardly moved when he toted him from the airport to Nick's car. Yep, he would want a hearty breakfast this morning.

"Mr. Statham, we are within a couple of miles of your estate. The next turn to the left will be a winding road that will take us to your place."

The property was secured behind electric, sliding, high wooden gates, and when they passed through an elaborate carriage driveway, the enormous house and grounds were in full view from a distance. The grounds and gardens were beautifully maintained, and the house was exceptional.

When the car approached the front entrance, the door swung open, and a woman with white hair smiled and waved.

Nick honked the horn and gave a broad grin. "Ms. Greenwood, we have finally arrived with the hungry troops and hope you have a big breakfast prepared with plenty of tea!"

"Come, come. Bring the boys on in, and we shall have a feast!"

Al extended his hand to Ms. Greenwood and greeted her, then introduced her to Cole, who had just awakened. Do you come with our house, Ms. Greenwood?" Al inquired with a little chuckle.

"As a matter of fact, Mr. James has employed me part-time, but of course, this would be with your approval. Mr. Holland, would you like to show Mr. Statham and Cole around the lower level here while I place the finishing touches on our breakfast?"

"Yes, Ms. Greenwood. A dandy idea!"

The first level provided a continuation of the staircase onto the second and third floors. The master suite had a breathtaking vista of the rear gardens through a large feature window. The drapes were layered with assorted fabrics for daylight and night, which were operated electrically. The floors were white marble with plush and subtle-colored oriental rugs spread about with intention, and the furniture was mahogany at its finest. The ceilings were recessed, and the room had lovely angles with slight changes in the shade of paint. Al had never seen such extravagance. Attention had been given to every detail. It would take him weeks to absorb it all!

"Hey, Dad, I'm starving. Can we eat and then finish our tour?"

"You bet, son!"

Ms. Greenwood had prepared a variety of foods for their enjoyment. Cole said that the scones and homemade jams were the best. It brought back sweet memories for Al of Mayme's home-cooked meals and of course his lovely wife's wonderful dishes. In many ways, being out in the country seemed like a homecoming, and he found himself extremely comforted and his spirit quieted.

Cole excused himself from the table and softly mentioned he wanted to explore the rest of the house. "Oh yes, Ms. Greenwood, your breakfast was heavenly. Thank you so much for cooking for Dad and me!"

"Cole, it was my pleasure because I love to cook. Now, you run along, lad, and have a morning of new discoveries. Please let me know what you and your dad want for dinner. We'll have a proper meal in the dining room prepared at seven o'clock sharp. There are sandwich spreads in the cooler, and you may take your pick for lunch. Matter of fact, you boys are on your own for lunch. After I get the kitchen cleaned, I'll be spending several hours at my house. By way of the meadow, I live only a mile from here."

"Thanks again, Ms. Greenwood. We'll see you this evening, and Dad and I are not picky eaters, so anything you want to cook will be just fine with us."

Al was quick to reiterate that they had no meal preferences and were appreciative of having someone to prepare a few meals because he and Cole ate way too many hot dogs!

As Cole started up the stairs, he wondered who had previously lived in their house. As his hands slid over the finely polished wood of the banister, he experienced a sudden chill and wondered if there was some mystery to unravel within this house. He explored all of the second level and did not see a room that he would want as his.

When he reached the third level and saw the room straight across from the stairs, he knew it was his! One whole wall was a gorgeous mural of horses on the top of a mountain, cast against a magnificent sunset. There were beautiful bookcases with every book imaginable that a boy would want to read, and a work station with a large-screen computer. There were two sets of bunk beds with four full beds supported by the most exquisite massive wood, and on all four headboards there were beautifully hand-carved horses.

A handsome chest of drawers and plush rug were placed between the massive bunk beds. The walls were suede fabric rather than paint, and it felt so good to touch. His bathroom had a shower as large as a closet, and a colossal window where you could see the stables and meadow down below. There were two closets in his bedroom, and one of them was filled with riding apparel and boots.

Cole figured that Mr. James must have been responsible for the details of this room. To Cole, life had become a blur the last few weeks, and he longed to experience the day-to-day moments where he could have peaceful thoughts and pull the plug on constant changes. *Oh my Savior, slow us down; let us have time to be aware of your creation and enjoy the day you have made. Help us to go forward and not be reminded of our losses. This is a grand place, and I thank you for it, but, Lord, we need your substance in every part of our lives. I know my dad must feel the same way deep down. Please let us have a normal and quiet life, Lord. And, Lord, bring us friends and let them stay a part of our lives. Oh, Lord, I want a place to call home. Please keep us here.*

As he walked back downstairs, he again had an eerie feeling. He must remember to ask his dad about the history of this house.

After Al's tour of the house, he caught up with Cole at the stables, which felt more like where he belonged. He wondered why Richard had purchased a mansion for just the two of them. Perhaps it was a good investment with profits to be made in the future—or would it be a place for entertaining and promoting goodwill within the business? *Lord, help me place the future in your hands and live only in this moment with my precious son. We are grateful for your provision and protection, and, Lord, we do covet your guidance each and every day.*

"Dad, I found the tack room and just had a look at the riding gear; it is both English and western. Isn't that great? We can take our pick. But of course, I am only acquainted with western, and I do love it!"

"Cole, I will need a special tutor on how to converse with equestrian folks! This is all so foreign to me right now."

"Dad, you'll pick it up as we experience things together. Can't you see that country living is going to be good for us? We'll have fun exploring together on horseback!"

"Yes, and speaking of horses, I need to talk with Nick or perhaps Captain Conner about where to purchase a couple of gentle horses."

"I'm really tired, Dad. Let's go take a nap together. You can sleep on one of my bunk beds!"

"That sounds like a great idea."

Al slowly awakened and for a moment could not recall where he was until he saw the mural of the horses. The sun rays cast highlights that added a rich dimension to the painting. He looked over and breathed in the beautiful sight of his sleeping son, so peaceful and trusting. He reminded himself that this day was a new beginning, a new location, and there was no need for past baggage to haunt him. *Oh, my gracious Father, I am waiting before you and ask that you move our hearts' concerns and burdens so that we become yielded channels for you to work through. I am your child with outstretched arms for your help.*

A faint tinkle of a bell could be heard, and it seemed fairly persistent. Cole stirred and looked around, yawning. "Hey, Dad, could that be our call to dinner?"

"Let's check it out. I cannot believe we slept all afternoon!"

As they made their way down to the first floor, Ms. Greenwood welcomed them with a beautiful smile, and the smells from the kitchen and dining room could only be described as phenomenal.

"I have candles lit, table set, and serving bowls spread between the two of you. Now have a seat and just enjoy."

"Please, Ms. Greenwood, do join us," Al suggested.

"Another time, but for now, you boys need time to absorb your lovely home without having to entertain someone. I'm going to clean the kitchen and place some of the leftovers in the refrigerator. Oh yes, there is a lemon icebox pie in the refrigerator for a midnight snack. I'll be on my way back home in the next few minutes and will return in the morning. Cole, hope you like pancakes, bacon, and fruit! I'm going to bring some delicious maple syrup for the hotcakes in the morning."

"Ms. Greenwood, you are spoiling us. Actually, pancakes are my very favorite for breakfast. Aren't they, Dad?"

"Yep and mine, too!"

"Okay, boys, enjoy, and I'll see you in the morning."

As Al and Cole slowly ate their meal in quietness, each cherished the paths their imaginations had begun to travel. Cole had so many thoughts about the previous owners of the house, and Al was thinking how wonderful it would be if his lovely wife and daughter could have enjoyed such a place. But he knew in his heart they were in the loveliest of places and would not return even if they could. Maybe this was to be a little piece of heaven on earth.

"Cole, after dinner, let's take a walk down by the lake and watch the setting sun."

"Okay, Dad."

Cole was aware there was a strong presence in his room. The moon was shining through his window, and he could see and sense a shadowy form in the corner across from his bed.

"Who are you and what do you want from me?" *Dear Lord, if this is some kind of evil spirit, in the Name of Jesus, be gone!*

There was a small breeze that passed over his bed, and then the form was gone. Remaining still and quiet, except for his eyes, Cole remained in bed and wondered again about the previous master of this house. He finally drifted off into another deep sleep.

"Come up here and let's nap in the loft, Cole."

"No, I shall be carried away with your beauty, and you most certainly will dazzle me and lure me, and I must remain pure."

"Oh, Cole, do you not have any willpower whatsoever?"

"Not where you are concerned. I must not test the Lord, Nya."

"Cole, don't you ever feel lonely and just want to be held?"

"You know I have for years, Nya, but there will be a time when we can freely celebrate our love together with God's blessings, so, little girl, do not tempt me!"

"I shall leave then."

"Nya, please do not go."

He watched her run through the meadow and into the woods, and again he was wide awake. As he pondered the dream, he could not help but wonder if this was a vision of some future event. It seemed so real …

Somewhere in the distance, Al heard a rooster crow. He smiled to himself and shouted, "What a wonderful country sound!" He leaped out of bed as though he were sixteen years old. He pressed the button for the curtains to open and inhaled majestic expectations for this new day.

As he walked down the long hall, he could hear Ms. Greenwood's beautiful voice. She was singing "Victory in Jesus." *Oh, God, what a glorious day. Thank you, sweet Jesus.*

"Good morning, Ms. Greenwood, and how are you?"

"I am doing very well—and yourself?"

"Could not be better!"

"Did you and Cole get any sleep after that long nap yesterday?"

"We retired before ten, and I slept like a baby. Haven't seen Cole yet, but I cannot imagine anything interrupting his beauty rest!"

"Have a seat, Al, and perhaps we can chat a few minutes before Cole comes to join us for breakfast. I wanted to tell you about the previous master of the house."

"Please do. I wondered why our company chose to purchase such a large estate for just Cole and me. Perhaps it came as a bargain?"

"I would think so, because it had been vacant for a while. You see, the owner was a businessman like yourself, and he had a young wife and child. He traveled most of the time, and servants were hired to take care of the house and grounds. I did not work here but had an acquaintance who did. Anyway, the previous owner's name was Evan Strickland. His wife was named Lisa, and their little girl was Nya. I was told that one morning Ms. Lisa was found dead in one of the guest bedrooms on the second floor. Mr. Strickland had arrived home unexpectedly the night before, and there had been quite an argument between the two, and little Nya had witnessed it, along with one of the servants. Apparently, Ms. Lisa took an overdose of pills and died during the night. From all accounts, there was no history of domestic violence, so the death of Ms. Lisa was a surprise to the entire community. Mr. Strickland nearly drowned in his grief, and in less than a year vacated this property and bought a modest home several miles from here. I hear that he still travels and rarely comes home to see his daughter. Ms. Lisa had a sister, and she now cares for the child entirely. I believe Nya is around twelve or thirteen."

"That is quite a story and indeed a very sad one."

"Good morning, Ms. Greenwood!"

Cole wrapped his arms around his dad and sat down beside him.

"Well, son, what's on your mind this morning?"

"I had an interesting visitor in my room last night."

Ms. Greenwood's eyes got big, and Al was quietly waiting for an explanation.

"Okay, this is what happened. I awoke knowing that something was in the corner of my room. I've thought about it this morning and have come to the conclusion it was a spirit or an angel. And then there is something else. I had a dream that was so real. I was in the dream, and there was a girl named Nya. That is a strange and unique name and one I've never heard before, but I'm positive the girl in my dream was Nya, and we were well acquainted. Actually, we were grown. Since I had the dream about the airplane incident, I'm wondering if this dream may have a future meaning, too. What do you make of this, Dad?"

"You've thrown me a curve, Cole, and this is something I'll need to ponder."

"Ms. Greenwood, what is your take?"

"Cole, you are an extremely intuitive young man, and I would never discount your dreams. I tend to agree with your dad. I'll need time to digest what you've shared."

"I say we have some of your pancakes, Ms. Greenwood. Dad and I have a day of adventure ahead of us. Don't we, Dad?"

"I'll say. Life is always an adventure with you, son!"

---

Vera came rushing into Dana's office, danced around her desk, and waved the newspaper up in the air before plopping it down beside Dana's cup of coffee.

"What's this little jig all about, Vera?"

"Your guy, Al. Just have a look at the front page!"

Dana stared in disbelief. How could this be? How could one modest individual be involved in so many high-profile events in such a short time? This was absolutely unreal.

"Well, what do you think, Dana? Certainly, not your typical criminal, right?"

"I never said he was, and I resent the liberty you are taking in this conversation, Vera."

"I am so sorry. Please accept my humble apology."

"Apology accepted. Truly, it seems that Al is favored by the gods. Who would have thought that the opinion of the public and the media could question a man's innocence and then days later sing praises to their new hero?"

"Dana, this is astounding, is it not?"

"Seems he has a knack for saving people's lives these days. Just wish it had been the same twenty years ago."

"Well, I for one think that he saved his own life twenty years ago. I believe your guy has always had a good heart but perhaps was misguided and misdirected when he was younger."

"Why do you call him my guy?"

"Because it is obvious that you have strong feelings for him and have been unduly upset since you learned he was moving to another country."

"That is very true, but Al and I are simply not on the same page, Vera."

"Since Mr. Davidson felt strongly about another interview with Al, I would be happy to interview him for you, Dana."

"I'm not sure the company would pay for you to fly to England even if Al were to consent to be interviewed."

"I've been with the company longer than you, Dana, and I do feel that I've learned more than just the basics where interviews are concerned. And you must admit I've handled your workload pretty well since you've been unmotivated lately. I know I'm being extremely candid, but perhaps I could handle Al's story well enough until you feel more like yourself again. Just think about it. You could take the information I gather and write another article to absolutely ensure your climb up the corporate ladder. Right?"

Up until Vera's last statement, Dana had resented much of what she was suggesting, but perhaps Vera's fact-finding venture could be just the ticket for another raise and even another promotion. Financial security was constantly on her mind, especially since she wanted to help her family.

"You know, Vera, you may have a good idea here. If you were to go to England in my stead, it would give me a chance to get my head cleared and also do some groundwork in other areas of interest. I have seen a few interesting articles in other magazines where I could dig a bit deeper and perhaps target further interest and bring in more profits for our company by piggybacking. I will talk with Mr. Davidson in the morning, okay?"

"Sounds good to me! I've never been to England!"

"And I've never had a desire to go to such a dreary place … not enough sunshine!"

"Well, there's your answer. You do not want to go, and I am willing!"

———❧———

Captain Conner, Al, and Cole had been visiting some of the local landowners who raised horses and sold them. Most of the horses they had seen were gentle saddle horses, and their gaits were as smooth as honey. Al was quickly catching on to how to navigate these pleasure-riding horses and found that riding was almost second nature. Of course Cole was totally at home on all of the horses he rode, even the more spirited ones.

"Well, Al, have you and Cole grown fond of any of these steeds yet?"

"Captain, I'll let Cole be the judge of that."

"Well, Cole, what do you think?"

"I believe I'll know immediately when we should buy a horse, and I have not met the right one yet!"

"We have one more place to visit today, and I know you'll remember the lady we shall visit next. She is an airline stewardess part-time and horsewoman full-time. Remember Ms. Joseph who was on your flight?"

"Wow, Captain Conner, how could we forget?"

Al shook his head and smiled in a bashful manner. "I think the world gets smaller all the time! Yes, we remember India Joseph—and what a pleasant young woman. We would love an opportunity to reconnect with Ms. Joseph and check out the horses she has for sale!"

Cole was beaming, and Al was equally thrilled at this turn of events.

Captain Conner gave a little laugh. "You guys must have *really* been impressed with Ms. Joseph."

"How far does she live from our place, Captain?"

"Only a few miles, and if these horses are suitable, we will not need a trailer to transport them to your place. Cole and I can ride them, and, Al, you can drive my truck. Doesn't get easier than that!"

"Oh, Dad, look at the green pastures and white fence! Most places here have the stone fences, but I personally love the white against the lush green. What a great place to ride horses!"

"India lives in a modest home and takes care of her niece. I think you'll find the place most inviting. The stables are much larger than the house, and India has a part-time trainer to break the horses and watch over their health. His name is Robby. He loves horses, and one would think they were his family. Whenever you have an opportunity to meet him, you'll instantly like him."

As they drove up to the stables, India was waiting to greet them. "Hey, guys, welcome to our humble abode."

"Ms. Joseph, these are grand stables!"

"Cole, you are so kind. It is great to see you and your dad. I've thought about you two quite a few times since our flight together and hope you've recovered from the trauma and found your home to be all you expected."

Al stepped up and took India's hand in his and held it for a moment in appreciation of all she had done for Cole. He could never thank her enough for extending herself to both of them. She had such class—but more importantly, grace.

"Okay, I hope you'll trust the liberty I've taken to select two horses for you to view and ride. I do believe these will be a great pair together. They are very different, and I believe one is well suited for Cole and the other for you, Al. Cole, I'm going to bring Mystery out first. How do you like that name?"

"It is interesting. Guess I will never know what's on her mind, right?"

"Oh, you assumed she was a mare?"

"I don't think guys are mysterious. Do you?"

She laughed and said, "No comment."

Mystery was a sleek grayish white mare with a smoky colored mane, tail, and stockings. Her head was perfect with small ears and a dark gray nose. Her neck had a beautiful arch, and her eyes were a blue gray. She was the most beautiful creature Cole had ever seen, and he was already taken with her. She came right up to Cole and Al and gave Cole a little nudge.

"May I ride her, Ms. Joseph?"

"Well, of course. I saddled her up and raised the stirrups just for you. Here, let me give you a boost up to the stirrup on her left side. I'm sure you are aware that you mount from the horse's left side, right?"

"I am. My teacher taught me many things regarding safety and how to help my horse have confidence in my ability."

"Spoken like a real professional."

"Okay, here we go. How do you feel in this saddle?"

"It is just right. How did you know?"

"I've been around the block a few times, sweet lad. Follow me to the corral, and I'll give you plenty of time to get to know Mystery. She has wonderful gaits, and her canter is the smoothest I've experienced. Take your time getting to know her, and she'll be a pleasure to ride. We'll return soon after I get your dad's horse."

Cole knew immediately this was the horse he wanted and would love forever! Her hair felt like satin on her neck, and she had such a strong neck. She carried herself like royalty. Cole was in total command, and Mystery seemed pleased to have him on her back.

"Al, what do you think so far?"

"I am overwhelmed, India, and can hardly wait to see the horse you've selected for me."

"I'll be right back. He is majestic, and I believe will be well suited for you, Al."

India returned with a larger horse, black in color with a thick, long, wavy mane and tail that dragged along the ground. His head was held high, and his coat looked as soft as velvet. He was absolutely magnificent in every way.

"Okay, Al, let's walk up to the corral, and I'll hold him until you've mounted. I know he looks to be perhaps a little spirited, but he is gentle as a lamb. Trust me—I've been around him since he was born, and he is a big pet."

She opened the gate, and Samson and Mystery were excited to be by each other's side. They were an exquisite pair and seemed to be made for each other.

Al was pleasantly surprised how easily his horse obeyed his commands, little that he knew. Actually, Samson was guiding Al or perhaps teaching him. The four spent the next hour riding together in the pastures and jumping over a few narrow creeks at Cole's lead. The rhythm of the two was like ballroom dancing, and Al found himself feeling totally liberated and enjoying himself with his son as never before. *Oh my heavenly Father, you are so perfect in your sovereignty, and I worship you this glorious day.*

*Thank you again for this new beginning. Take us on a journey that will glorify you.*

As they approached the stables, India knew in her heart of hearts the four were meant to be. These two horses were her pride and joy, and she could have never released them to just a buyer. Samson and Mystery had to be sold to extraordinary people, and she knew Al and Cole would care for these horses forever.

As Cole's face beamed, he could hardly wait to say, "We've found our horses!"

"I hope money is no object, but if it is, I shall give Samson and Mystery to you, for they were born to be yours!"

"We appreciate your gesture, India, but we came prepared to pay top dollar. Will you take a personal check or shall I get a cashier's check?"

"Your check will be great!"

"Captain, you've been rather quiet. What do you think?"

"I think they are keepers! Let's get this show on the road, gang! Are we ready to ride the horses to your place, Al?"

"Why not. Are you ready to ride Samson and let Cole follow on Mystery?"

"I am, and here are the truck keys. We'll get a head start while you settle up with India."

Al and India watched Conner and Cole until they were out of sight. Al felt strangely drawn to India. Although he could not put his finger on it, she reminded him of Cindy and stirred something in him that had been untouched since Cindy's death.

"Come with me to our house, Al, and we'll settle up. I would like for you to meet my niece, Nya."

"And your niece would be just now entering into the teenage years, right?" "Precisely and how would you have knowledge of such?"

"'Tis another story for another time."

"As you wish."

The small house was welcoming, and the ferns and flowers that cloaked the little cottage made it seem alive. There was a loft with a single window in the front, and a small girl could be seen looking down.

"Come, Al. I'll introduce you to Nya."

As Al entered the house, there was a delicate fragrance that magically appealed to his senses, one of spices and citrus that delighted his very soul. Nya glided down the beautifully crafted spiral staircase with amazing grace and poise. She was a slight little thing with enormous crystal-blue eyes and skin fairer than the fairest. In no way could he see that she resembled her aunt, but there was the same level of confidence that each possessed. As he recalled Cole's dream, he was sure in his spirit that this relationship would be significant.

"Nya, I would like for you to meet Mr. Statham. He is purchasing Mystery and Samson today, and he and his son, Cole, live only a few miles from us."

"Good morning, Mr. Statham. I'm confident you are indeed a special individual for my aunt to part with Mystery and Samson, for they are her heartbeat, and we both shall miss them sorely."

"Good to meet you, Nya, and you and India must come visit us frequently and stay connected with your beloved horses."

"Nya, Mr. Statham has a son around your age, so perhaps you could show him around on horseback. He will find some of the forest areas and streams most enjoyable to explore. And you as well, Al. We could meet halfway in the early morning and enjoy riding while the horses do not have to labor in the heat. We have found the forests in this area to be absolutely enchanting."

"Since I will be on vacation for a month or so, your plan sounds perfect for us, India. Now, what is your fee for the new addition to our family?"

"Did Conner give you any idea about the cost of this breed?"

"Nothing other than it would be a lifetime investment of pleasure and money!"

"Mystery and Samson together will be $20,000."

"And I suppose that is a bargain?"

"No, actually a miracle, for I had never intended to sell either of them."

"We are honored and grateful, India. You must fulfill your part of the contract and come visit regularly."

"We will once you've had a few more days to settle in. Actually, there is a path that Nya discovered that brings us to your property line. All we need is a gate, and we shall be connected!"

"I'll personally take care of that as soon as possible!"

As Al departed down the long driveway, he watched the two of them in the rearview mirror of the truck until the tiny figures disappeared in the distance. *Oh my Lord, what an impact these two little women have made upon my heart. Without any doubts, you have brought these angels into our lives, and how I praise your name. Your design has wings of angels and ancient spirits. Oh, Lord, how majestic are your ways.*

———— ✶✶✶✶✶✶✶ ————

Ms. Greenwood had left a local newspaper on the kitchen table before she departed to go home for the day. Al surmised it was so he could read that the good folks of the community were grateful for his heroic act at the airport. It had been close to two weeks, and he had avoided seeing all newspapers until now. There had been a call from Nat Germany requesting an interview for the community paper of Leeds, but he had not returned Nat's call. And oddly enough, there was a message left the previous day regarding an interview request with the *Entrepreneur*. If he remembered correctly, it was Dana's assistant. People are always searching for the truth, but most have blinders and are unable to recognize it. *Lord, we must be born again to really recognize the truth. And to be born again is to immediately die to self. Lord, we may be in this world, but praise your name, we do not have to be partakers of it! Thank you, Father, for opening my eyes to the truth.*

"Hey, Dad, are you coming for our morning ride?"

"Don't think so this morning, son. There are a couple of people who have called and left messages, and I need to return their calls. One of them is Ms. Dana's assistant. Wouldn't it be wonderful if Ms. Dana could visit?"

"That would be awesome, Dad. Please invite her!"

"Not to concern yourself. I will."

"Okay, then I'm off and shall explore on my own. I may not be back for lunch, so I'm taking snacks with me. Mystery and I will miss you and Samson. This will be our first ride alone."

"Be careful, Cole, and enjoy yourself."

"Okay, Dad. I love you."

"Love you too, son."

Cole headed to the back of the property where a new gate had recently been constructed to allow passage back to Mystery's original home. He wondered if she missed her former family. Today would be a good time to weave through the forests, jump over narrow streams and creek beds, and eventually meander back over to Ms. Joseph's place. He remembered how kind she was to him when he was separated from his dad at the airport. Cole felt strangely drawn to Ms. Joseph.

"Slow down, Mystery. We'll get there, girl!"

They came to a halt, and Cole heard a branch snap. He looked up and to his surprise saw a figure at the top of a mossy knoll right across the stream beside them. He waited and watched for the figure to move, but the only movement was the girl's long hair being blown across her face.

"Hello down there!"

Cole waved his hand and continued to wait. Slowly, the girl wove her way down the embankment and jumped across the stream at its narrowest point. When she approached Mystery, the mare stretched her neck and tugged on the reins and then stepped forward toward the girl.

"Hey, Mystery, I've missed you, too."

"So you know Mystery?"

"Yes, and I've heard all about you, Cole, and your dad, too!"

"I was actually thinking about riding to Ms. Joseph's place so Mystery could see her former home."

"That would be my home, too. Ms. Joseph is my aunt India. My name is Nya!"

Cole remained silent.

"Are you feeling okay, Cole?"

"I'm not sure."

"Here, let me help you dismount."

The dream was coming back to Cole, and he could see that Nya favored the older girl in his dream. *Lord, I'm not sure I understand the purpose of these dreams that give me a glimpse of the future. I do not have the maturity or the wisdom to decipher such. Please help me, Jesus.*

"Have a seat on this nice grassy spot, and I'll bring some cool water over from the stream."

She cupped water in both of her hands and gently poured it over Cole's head and face. "Now, does that help? You don't look quite so pale."

"It does help."

"Well, you looked as if you had seen a ghost."

"I did."

"Where?"

"In my room when we first moved into our house!"

"Do you really believe in ghosts?"

"Not really, but I do believe in supernatural happenings, don't you?"

"I believe there is a mighty God who controls everything."

"Do you believe that Jesus is God's Son?"

"I believe that He is Son of God and Son of man. Now that we've waded through the serious stuff, can we be friends?"

Cole smiled and said, "Yes, we can."

"Why don't we go to our house and let Mystery see all of her friends while we get a bite to eat and make some homemade ice cream?"

"You actually know how to make ice cream?"

"I do, and it's easy enough to teach you!"

———✦———

Al and Cole had many things to converse about over dinner, and what a fine meal Ms. Greenwood had prepared! There was a fresh chicken, baked and seasoned with herbs from their herb garden, green beans with green onions and toasted almonds, creamed corn from Ms. Greenwood's garden, and yeast rolls. They had gotten spoiled so quickly, especially by the desserts, and tonight there was a fresh coconut cake that both of them kept eyeing at the end of the dining room table.

"I'm telling you, Dad, meeting up with Nya today was an emotional encounter. I know you believe God has given me a gift of prophecy through my dreams, but you have to know this is pretty weighty stuff for a thirteen-year-old!"

"Soon to be fourteen, son. You are becoming a young man and one that our God has already begun to use for His purposes."

"Why can't things be simple in our lives, Dad?"

"Because God wants us to be involved in His work, and He gives us God- sized assignments when we are willing vessels."

"Putting aside my assignment for God, I must say I had a marvelous time with Nya. She taught me so much that I did not know about horses, plus many tips on how to make custard and ice cream. It is really remarkable how keeping things simple can produce the tastiest food. I guess being around a girl expands a boy's horizons, right?"

Al could no longer contain his amusement and laughed until he cried. At first Cole was not sure how to take it, but soon their conversation was sprinkled with laughter and pure joy.

"Dad, let's walk out to the lake after we clean the dishes and watch the sunset."

"I believe that is becoming a ritual of ours."

———

That night before falling asleep, Al revisited the conversations and events of the day. He had called Nathaniel Germany, a reporter for the *British Daily News*. Nat was such a kind young man and seemed sincere in wanting to write an article that could shed positive light on the outcome of the plane crash, rather than the airline and pilot being bashed. Al had mentioned that it may not be newsworthy since so much time had lapsed, but Nat said it would be good for the community of Leeds as well as the airlines and Captain Conner. They made an appointment for Nat to come out to the house the following week.

Al had also returned Vera's call. Their conversation had a surprising twist to it. Vera Parker was not calling on behalf of Dana but for herself. Dana had declined doing a follow-up interview because of a heavy workload and insisted that Vera come in her stead. It came to him in a flash—why not have both reporters do their interviews at the same time! Al preferred not to be interviewed, but if this would work for the greater good of God's purposes, then so be it. *Oh Father, help me to stay focused on the moments of simplicity each and every day with Cole, and at the same time, please give me discernment to see things from a heavenly perspective, knowing that it is your will, not mine.*

———

India and Nya had talked and sipped on herbal tea until the wee hours of the night. Nya seemed to have more questions about her mom since apparently Cole had witnessed some kind of spirit in his bedroom.

She had no desire to go back to her former home. In fact, it was her worst nightmare. Aunt India was always reluctant to share much about her sister, Lisa, but as time marched on, Nya became more inquisitive; naturally, she wanted to know about her mother from a grown-up's perspective. She was forever playing in her head the last time she and her mom and dad were together …

Prior to her dad's arrival home that evening, she and her mom and Robby were having tea and pastries. The conversation was delightful and lighthearted, and her mom seemed so young and happy. She knew her mom was lonesome much of the time because her dad traveled and came home only on rare occasions. They had not expected him home for another day, and when he came into the kitchen and saw them laughing and eating together with Robby, he went into a rage. This was where Nya always stopped herself from thinking any further because it made her dislike her father.

Her thoughts immediately turned to the day with Cole. He was such a good student and had a thirst for knowledge. But in many ways, he was wise beyond his years and was unaware of his old spirit. For some reason, she thought of him as a young modern-day prophet, and she sensed in her spirit that he would be a vibrant part of her life. After he told her about his two recent dreams, she knew God's hand was upon him. She invited him to go to the little community church she and her aunt attended, and he seemed genuinely happy about the prospect. Since her mom died, she had prayed for God to bring someone into her life that she could count on. Aunt India worked part-time, but truth be known, she was preoccupied full-time with her profession. Nya had wondered many times if she would always be as lonesome as her mother had been. She believed her dad took all the blame for her mother's death, and whenever he came home, she could tell he was guilt-ridden. He stayed only long enough to have an evening meal and make small talk. Long after she had gone to bed on those evenings, she could hear Aunt India talking with him until midnight or after, and at times it seemed she heard her dad crying. She had a remarkable resemblance to her mom, and she could tell her dad found this disturbing every time he looked upon her. There was so much she did not know, but perhaps in time it would be sorted out—or it would not matter.

# Chapter 3

Vera unlocked the front door, set her computer and purse down on the foyer table, placed the bag of food on the kitchen table, and went directly in to check on her mother. Her mom had been in ill health for two years, and the only diagnosis was congestive heart failure. Vera's dad had died of a heart attack when she was sixteen, and since that time, she had witnessed her mom's health slowly deteriorating.

Vera had received a full scholarship to Columbia University in New York when she finished high school. Although she really did not want to leave her mom, she knew that a scholarship to a college like Columbia would give her advantages in her career that she could not pass up. She remained there until getting her master's degree and then returned home to St. Louis.

Her first job was at the *Herald*, and she loved it. She had an opportunity to learn from reporters and journalists she had long admired. She felt comfortable living back in the house with her mom. It seemed to work well for both of them. After a couple of years at the *Herald*, she wanted to connect more with people rather than events, so she decided to initiate an interview at the *Entrepreneur*. Their magazine had only been marketed for a year or so when it caught her eye. She liked their promotion of the positive aspect of people's experiences and events, and she also found it remarkable that their foundation seemed to be one of integrity, if indeed that could be said of the media. It took more than a month for her to get an interview after contacting them and forwarding her resume. She was hired during her interview and started working in a pool of other journalists two weeks later. After a year, she was given a handsome raise and promoted to Dana Fulton's assistant. Dana had a great reputation for her creative writing, but since getting personally involved with a client, her lack of concentration and focus had stymied her creative ability.

Vera felt sorry for Dana and really did want to help her get through this slump. They could do this together. Actually, the two of them were close to the same age, and Vera had looked forward to working closely with someone she could share more than just business related things. What she really wanted to have was an opportunity to share Christ with Dana! She had seen firsthand that pride could blind one from seeing the truth. *Oh dear Lord, when we are tempted to think of our dignity, our triumphs, and rights, we need to revisit Jesus washing His disciples' feet. Sweet Jesus, you have the love to see what we can be and the power to help us attain it. Where would I be without your truth and mercy?*

"Hey, Mom, I have so much to tell you this evening! Are you up for coming to the table and visiting over dinner?"

"I was just thinking about how I would enjoy a nice long visit with you, sweetheart."

"Have you been up and around during the day, or has it been mostly a down day for you, Mom?"

"Surprisingly, I've felt up to washing a couple of loads of clothes and even pressing a few of your white blouses."

"Mom, I wish you would not tax yourself. I do not mind taking my cotton tops to be pressed at the cleaners. I would rather you expend your energy on more enjoyable things."

"Not to fret, I had a good day!"

"Please come and sit down while I serve our food. I stopped by the little corner deli and got us some boiled shrimp, French bread, slaw, and a slice of chocolate pie for each of us. Sound good?"

"Sounds heavenly. I have an enormous appetite this evening!"

"That's not the norm for you, so we'll take advantage of this hallelujah good time, Mom!"

"Give me your hand, sweetie, and I'll say our blessing. Dear Lord in heaven, what a gracious heavenly Father you are. We are so thankful for this food and ask you to bless it to our bodies. I ask you to always protect my sweet daughter, and I covet your favor for her. Please keep us mindful that the only way is the way to the cross, for truly it leads home. Please continue to use Vera for your kingdom purpose and let her shine for you in word and deed. We are always at your mercy, Father, and we desire your Presence more than our very breath. Thy will be done. Amen."

"Thank you, Mom, for such a beautiful blessing and prayer. I love when you pray over us. It gives me great comfort."

"Never forget what a companion you always have in the Holy Spirit, for we are constantly revived and renewed by the workings of the Spirit. We are never alone, no matter what kind of challenges spring up for us to embrace. We must always remember to ask the Holy Spirit to speak true wisdom to our beings so we will remain cross-centered. Jesus offers us glory, but He offers us a cross as well. More than anything, I pray that our Lord would give you fresh revelations daily as you read your Bible. Just remember Jesus' unconditional love and commitment surrounds those that God has given Him. You will never be alone."

"Mom, are you trying to tell me you're not going to be with me much longer?"

"Sweetheart, we never know when God will call us home, but right now, I feel really great and desire to have a feast with you tonight!"

After they had finished up the last bite of the chocolate pie, Vera cleared the table while her mom listened attentively about the prospect of her daughter making a trip to England. Both were excited and knew this would be a grand opportunity for Vera. It had been one of their best times together in a while. She had not witnessed her mom being this energetic in the last couple of years. She was also relieved that her mom gladly gave her blessings regarding the trip to England, should it materialize.

"Okay, Mom, let's get you to bed. Let's both change into our PJs and read some scripture before retiring. I'm going to check my messages and then I'll be back to tuck you in."

"Take your time; I'm not sleepy in the least. And, sweetheart, thank you for the wonderful meal and our time together tonight. You are the best, and this mother loves you so much."

"I love you more!"

Dana had procrastinated long enough. She picked up the phone and placed a call to Al.

"Hello, this is the Statham residence. May I help you?"

"Would Mr. Statham happen to be in? This is Dana Fulton calling."

"Please hold for a moment, and I will check for you." Ms. Greenwood came back shortly and said, "Ms. Fulton, they have already left for the stables. I'm so sorry. May I take your number and have Mr. Statham give you a call when he returns?"

"He already has my number but please ask him to call at his earliest convenience."

"Yes, I will do that. Goodbye, Ms. Fulton."

Maybe she needed a little more time before talking with Al. Just thinking about it made her heart race. She knew she was being selfish thinking about her own feelings right now, but could not help herself. Vera's mother, Mrs. Parker, had passed away two nights ago, and her service would be held in the morning. The only family Vera had left was an uncle and a cousin.

After knocking softly on Dana's office door, Vera entered. "Good morning, Dana. How are you?"

"Oh, Vera, come let me give you a hug. I am so very sorry about your mother."

"Thanks, Dana. All of this is like a dream, so unexpected. I'm thankful there have been so many details to handle because it has kept me too busy to think or feel."

"Please have a seat, Vera. I want you to know I will do whatever I can to help you in any way. Matter of fact, I just put a call through to Al Statham. I was going to share with him that since your mom has passed away, we need to postpone your trip. Actually, I suppose I could go since you'll need time to handle your mom's business affairs."

"Dana, that's not necessary. Mom's life has simplified itself over the last few years, and there is no estate to settle, especially since I'm the only child. I would still love to have an opportunity to travel to England, but I do request we reschedule my appointment with Mr. Statham. Give me an extra week, and I will be prepared to take on the assignment. What do you say?"

"That sounds like a plan. After I talk with Al, I'll reschedule your flight and give you the details. I want you to take care of your personal matters this next week. I've already talked with Mr. Davidson about some temporary help for the time you'll be out of the office, and he's in full agreement. Just concentrate on things at hand right now. Oh, Vera, I'm truly sorry for your loss. Please know I'm here for you. Also, you may need company since you've been accustomed to living with your mom, and I would love to have you come stay with me."

"Oh, Dana, you are so very kind. Isn't it strange how difficult circumstances can bring people together? A week ago, our minds were riveted on the future of this company and our careers, and now our hearts are intertwined because of my profound loss. Life is ever so fragile, and we need to live in the moment and know our great God is in control of all things in our lives."

"You sound like Al. The two of you have a peaceful posture in seemingly all things that life tosses your way, even the most wounding hardships. I am truly amazed. I wish I were more accepting of difficult and challenging circumstances, but unfortunately, I tend to worry, analyze, and attempt to solve. How is that you and Al have an immediate resolve regarding adversity?"

"Maybe it's because we know in our heart of hearts that God is in total control and has plans to give us a good life and carry us in His peace regardless of our circumstances. It is a decision one makes at some point. I think perhaps the turning point of my life was when my dad died. My mom was so dependent upon him, and he was the rock in our lives. Gradually, I saw my mom learn to abide and not strive, and witnessing God's comforting and healing touch in her life showed me plainly that I could trust my heavenly Father in all things. Even though we shall lose our loved ones, Jesus will never forsake us. He is our constant companion."

"Oh, Vera, you and Al are indeed on the same page. Listening to you is like sitting here having a conversation with Al. I hope one day I can walk in the same grace as you two."

# Chapter 4

Al was enjoying the first and perhaps best event of the day … a cup of coffee in the fresh air, alone with God and his own thoughts. He had established this little ritual some weeks back. There was a beautifully hand-carved wooden bench that positioned one to have full view of the beautiful rear gardens. *Lord, you've been so gracious to simplify our lives in the past couple of weeks, and I thank you for answering my prayers. I coveted this reprieve. Cole is happier than I have witnessed since the death of his mom, and I know you, oh God, are healing, restoring, and renewing our spirits. Everything is in your timing, and thank you for letting me rest in your peace, sweet Jesus.*

The interview with Nat had gone extraordinarily well, and the article that was written and distributed to many papers throughout England had focused on the positives around Al's life and his business. He was so thankful to be settling down in a community that so graciously welcomed him. Richard had called a few days after the interview with Nat was published, and they chatted for a while about the company's direction, profits, and how Al would be welcomed into the Halifax office and reenter the business seamlessly. Richard suggested that Al's sabbatical be extended until Cole was settled in school, and this was such a relief to Al. He had been thinking about asking Richard to extend his time off, and God had worked it out so beautifully.

Dana's assistant, Vera, had flown in the day before and was settled in the guest quarters on the second floor. He had mentioned to Dana when she called to postpone Vera's trip that lodging reservations would not be necessary, and at his request, Ms. Greenwood would be staying full-time during Vera's visit as well. He had instinctively known Ms. Greenwood might be a comfort to Vera during this time of grief over the loss of her mom. Even though the little inn close by was welcoming, it hurt Al's heart to think of Vera grieving alone in a strange place.

"Good morning, Mr. Statham."

"Hello, Vera. Trust you rested well last night and Ms. Greenwood has made you feel most welcomed this morning."

"I could not be more comfortable, and already I adore Ms. Greenwood. We have been preparing our breakfast together, and I feel as though I have known her all my life!"

"Excellent. That is welcomed news! I have had my reservations about the company purchasing such a large place for just Cole and me, but it seems to be working out nicely to have plenty of room for guests, especially with the grace that our devoted Ms. Greenwood extends."

"She is indeed an asset, Mr. Statham."

"Vera, would you mind calling me Al? I have never felt comfortable being addressed as Mr. Statham. It seems much too proper and stiff."

"Okay, then I shall call you Al."

"All right."

"How's your appetite this morning?"

"Let's see. I'm thinking pancakes and scones would be wonderful with homemade jams and fresh maple syrup, and some crisp bacon on the side!"

"How did you know what we had prepared?"

"I put in my request yesterday morning before your arrival!"

"Ms. Greenwood is so very fond of you and your son."

"We love her as well. She is gracious, loyal, and devoted to our household. Not sure we could manage without her."

Al stood up and linked his arm with Vera's as they made their way to the kitchen.

The dining room table was set for a king. Ms. Greenwood had the fine china, sterling silver, and crystal glasses perfectly placed, plus a centerpiece of freshly cut roses from the garden. It was picture-perfect, and every place setting was surrounded with small crystal serving plates of pancakes, scones, and bacon. The "boarding house" reach had been eliminated entirely.

"Ms. Greenwood, we are so glad you are joining us for breakfast this morning. I believe this is your first time, but it will not be the last. The table and your preparations are beautiful. Cole and I appreciate all you do for us."

"I had plenty of help this morning, and from our guest at that!"

"I enjoyed every moment," Vera said as she lightly touched Ms. Greenwood's shoulder.

"Good morning, everyone," Cole said with a big smile as he entered the dining room.

"Cole, you were still at the stables yesterday evening when Ms. Vera arrived and settled in the guest quarters. Vera, this is my son, Cole—and, Cole, this is Ms. Vera, who works with Ms. Dana in America!"

"It is a pleasure to meet you, Ms. Vera."

"Thank you, Cole, and I am delighted to make your acquaintance."

"I miss Ms. Dana so much. Have you seen her lately?"

"Yes, I have, and she is quite well."

"That's good to know. I was really hoping she would come visit us."

"I'm sure she will soon, Cole. She is very busy right now with her new position, but I'm confident she'll get some time off this next year."

"Ms. Vera, do you like to ride horses?"

"I've always thought about riding horses but never had the chance. Are you up for teaching an old student?"

"You bet I am!"

"Hey, Dad, do you think Samson is gentle enough for Ms. Vera to ride?"

"You are the professional horseman, son, and you can better answer that question than I."

"Then I would say yes! When do you want to start your lessons?"

"After breakfast?"

"Oh, yes, and I know just the place we'll visit today!"

With a quick smile, Al said, "Don't suppose it would be where a certain girl named Nya lives?"

"She is my best friend ever, and we can also teach Ms. Vera how to make home-made ice cream!"

Vera chuckled and said, "I knew I was going to love England!"

After Vera and Cole set out to India's place, Al decided to give Captain Conner a call to inquire about the purchase of another horse. He discovered that Conner had recently acquired two new horses for himself. Conner had the day off and was going to load up the two horses and bring them by for Al to see.

Al never knew what each day held, and when Conner suggested a visit with two horses in tow, he braced himself for an active day with guests! He had instantly liked Vera Parker but in no way was looking forward to any type of interview. He hoped that she could visit a few days and gather facts for her magazine by observation only.

As Conner approached Al's place, he felt a strange sense of excitement in his spirit. He had instantly taken a liking to Al the first time he met him. Al was seemingly a man of integrity, courage, and pure common sense. Conner had never met a man such as Al. He also knew Al had not become the man he was by way of a soft and easy life. He knew today would be filled with immeasurable promise.

Al waved Conner in the direction of the corral so they could unload the horses.

"What a day of surprises, Conner! Seems my wish is your command!"

"It is all in the timing, Al, and you know what? You seem to have perfect timing in all things! This morning before you called, I was thinking that one horse was all I needed, especially to maintain wiggle room in the stables."

"Conner, are you becoming a shrewd businessman looking to turn a quick profit?"

"Now that you mention it, I would say yes!"

"Tell me about these two handsome creatures."

"The bay is a seven-year-old mare, and the buckskin is a five-year-old gelding. Both have been with the same rancher since birth. The mare was a steal because she is not a purebred, but the gelding is a quarter horse and has been trained. Even though he is young, he is very gentle and responsive. I believe he could be a nice addition for you."

"He is a beauty, indeed. I wish Mystery and Samson were here so we could make introductions, but they are headed to India's this morning."

"Who is the extra rider?"

"Actually, someone I would like to introduce to you. Her name is Vera

Parker, and she is from America. She flew over to interview me for the publisher she works for. It is a long story and one for a later conversation. Let's see if we can get a fresh pot of coffee brewed before Ms. Greenwood returns and wants to serve high tea!"

"How is it working out with Ms. Greenwood?"

"Could not be better. Never has there been a more kind and serving soul. Cole and I adore her, and she is dedicated to making our lives as pleasant as possible."

"That is great to hear, Al. You and Cole deserve to have your lives simplified. Now, tell me about this lady named Vera. You know a bachelor always needs to have options!"

"Oh, so you do have time for a relationship in your life!"

"I know I'm busy wearing many hats, but in my heart of hearts, I'm open for the right person in my life, Al."

"As am I."

---

Nya was with Robby in the stables feeding and grooming the horses. India would be flying in later that afternoon, and Nya wanted all the chores done so they could enjoy a meal together and discuss the things that mystified her. Robby had been a comfort to her since her mom died, and although he said little, she knew his thoughts were deep. Her dad had wanted to terminate Robby's employment after her mom died, but India talked him into letting him stay so there would not be further trauma in their lives. He was a great horse trainer and perhaps even a horse whisperer. He had a way with all animals. Her mother had employed him to teach them how to ride well, and after accumulating several horses, she realized that she needed daily help in the stables. Robby had grieved over her mother as much as she had.

"Nya, look who has come to visit," Robby said.

"Cole, we're in the stables!"

"Hi, Nya. Hi, Robby. This is Vera Parker riding with me today!"

As Robby neared Samson, the horse neighed gently and stepped forward to nuzzle him.

Vera said, "It is plain to see he misses you."

Robby and Nya unsaddled the horses after Cole and Vera dismounted and took them to the corral for water.

"We could go to the house and make some homemade peach ice cream. Who is in favor?" Nya asked.

"I can help," Vera said.

"Me, too," said Cole.

"Robby, you'll come along, right? You've helped me on many occasion with the ice and salt."

He smiled and nodded his head as Nya caught his hand and tugged.

"This is going to be the best ice cream ever because of the combined efforts of all these creative people. Are we a team or what?" asked Nya.

Vera laughed with abandon as they all headed to the house, and she knew in her heart it was going to be a very good day. How she needed some lighthearted moments ...

———————

"I guess it is settled then; we'll buy the buckskin!"

"Now, listen, Al, don't feel like I'm twisting your arm. He can easily be sold, so you do what works best for you."

"Okay, I've got a sweet deal for you, Conner. You leave the bay here during Vera's visit, so all four of us can ride together, and I'll make out a check to you this afternoon for the buckskin. By the way, does he have a name?"

"If he has one, I'm not aware of it, so what do you think? What suits him?"

"I think his name shall be Rapha!"

"I'm not familiar with the name. Do you know the meaning of it?"

"It means God has healed. And I truly feel that being settled here in Leeds has been a time of healing for me, Conner."

"You are a wise man, Al. Actually, you are a remarkable individual, and I thank God every day that you saved my life!"

"You would have done the same."

"By the way, are you going to church with the gang this Sunday? We could have Vera come along, too."

"That is a grand idea, and if I ask her to extend her stay, I'm confident she will. Do you have the day off tomorrow?"

"I do."

"Okay, it is settled. Come ready to ride tomorrow. I'll have Ms. Greenwood prepare breakfast for all of us, including her sweet self, and afterward the four of us can embark upon an adventure on horseback. You can lead the way. We'll have a bona fide trail ride! And I can promise you are going to fall in love with Vera Parker."

"Do I sense that you are fond of her?"

"I am, but my heart is drawn to India."

"I knew that when we went over to her place to purchase the horses. I could see that both of you were smitten!"

"Well, aren't you the matchmaker?"

"It looks as though we're two peas in a pod!"

They laughed until tears ran down Al's cheeks. It felt so good to really enjoy freedom. It was something he would never take for granted, for even though he did not go to prison, he had been locked away for many years in his mind. This was a grand day!

---

Cole awoke with his heart pounding loudly in his ears. He sat up and swung his feet to the floor and tried to remember the details of his dream. There was the sound of a crackling fire and horse stalls being kicked. It must be real. Could it be their stables? He ran down stairs and woke his dad.

"I'm headed to the stables. Something is on fire!"

"I'm right behind you, son!"

Upon arriving at the stables, all was quiet, except for Cole's heart pumping.

"Dad, this was one of those dreams that I know speaks of something that will happen. And right now, my heart is telling me it *is* happening! Could it be India's place or Conner's? Hurry, let's call them. Hurry, Dad!"

Al called India first and apologized for disturbing her but related that Cole's dream had urgency to it, and she needed to check the stables. Then he called Conner, and after only two rings, Conner answered and sounded wide awake. As Al was sharing Cole's dream, Conner dropped the phone. He could see the fire from his house.

Taking no thought of himself, only his precious horses, he ran to the stables and unlocked every stall. He yelled and clapped his hands, urging them to flee, and as the flames licked his naked legs, he saw the last horse to safety. His legs felt lit up like torches, but he had escaped, and his precious horses were saved. He lay on the ground shaking from shock and pain. He knew he needed to get himself to the hospital. *Oh, God, I need your help!* He drifted in and out of consciousness. He tried again to get up, and this time he knew He had God's strength. He managed to walk to the house and grab his keys and a blanket, and when he opened the door to leave, he heard Al calling his name.

———◦◦◦◦◦◦———

"Nya, Al called to give an update on Conner. He will need hospital care for the next few days, but he will have a complete recovery in time."

"Oh, Aunt India, I'm so relieved."

"Thank God for Cole. He is one gifted individual. I'm telling you, God has his hand on that child!"

"I don't see him as a child, Aunt India. I think because he is blessed with spiritual gifts, he is years ahead of his age. I'm thankful he is in our lives, aren't you?"

"Without a doubt, Cole and his dad are blessings straight from God. And I really like Vera. I can tell that she and Conner have connected. Did you notice he held her hand in church this past Sunday? And the fact that Al asked her to extend her stay was insightful on his part, don't you think?"

"The puzzle pieces are fitting together nicely. How I wish my dad could enjoy the fellowship of others. Do you think he will ever mellow, Aunt India?"

"Age, events, and the Holy Spirit can change quite a bit in an individual's life."

"I think your being on the same plane with Al and Cole has forever changed both of our lives."

"Yes, sweet girl, you are absolutely right."

There was a soft tap on the door as Robby entered and inquired about

Conner. "Ms. India, I would like to help Mr. Conner. Can you think of some way I might be helpful?"

"You know, Robby, you might be able to help Conner when he is discharged from the hospital. Certainly, you could have several hours off each day to go help Conner with errands or grocery shopping and some light cooking. We know firsthand what a good cook you are!"

"I can still take care of my responsibilities here and carve out a few hours for Conner on a daily basis, if this works for you. Nya, I'll need more help from you with the horses since we have Mr. Conner's with us now. Are you up for more chores?"

"Our vote is yes. Right, Nya?"

"You are absolutely correct, Aunt India!"

———————

Cole was still sleeping, and Ms. Greenwood was stirring around in the kitchen, so Al took his first cup of coffee and strolled out to the gardens to enjoy the glorious moments of God's new day. He was totally drained from the night's activities. He had stayed at the hospital with Conner until around 4:00. When he arrived home, Ms. Greenwood, Vera, and Cole met him at the front door. After relating what had happened, the three of them decided to try to get some sleep.

Al collapsed in his favorite chair in the living room and dozed for a couple of hours. Vera awakened him around six thirty, asking for directions to the hospital. She wanted to check on Conner and visit a couple of hours. Her flight back home was scheduled to leave that evening. He could see that she was conflicted in her spirit, and suspected she did not want to return home yet. He could relate to her grief over her mother and other pressing concerns. *Oh, Lord, we all need more courage, more trust in you, and to recognize this is not our home … we're just passing through, so light the pathway that you have designed for us to capture the joy in the moment through your Holy Spirit.*

Where was Nick Holland's number? It seemed amazing to him that one could accumulate so much in such a short time. Even though he was a neat and organized individual, his desk looked cluttered. After searching and opening and shutting drawers, Ms. Greenwood stepped around the corner and asked if she could help.

"Yes, thank you. I need Nick Holland's phone number and cannot locate it. Would you happen to have it or know where I can find a phonebook?"

"I have Nick's number in my address book; be back anon."

"Thanks so much."

"Here is Nick's number and a phonebook for your desk. I should have seen to getting a phone book for you earlier. Please accept my apology."

"There is no reason to apologize. You have since day one gone beyond the call of duty, Ms. Greenwood. Thank you for all you do and all that you are. We are in your debt, dear lady."

Al picked up the phone and called Nick's number.

"Hello, this is Nick here."

"Good morning, Nick. This is Al Statham."

"Oh, Mr. Statham, how are you doing? It is good of you to call."

"Nick, we are well and very blessed, but I am need of a favor. You are familiar with Captain Conner in our community, aren't you?"

"Yes, I know who you speak of. The guy who piloted your plane?"

"Correct. He had an unfortunate fire in his stables last night and is presently in the hospital with severe burns on both of his legs. He is going to recover, and certainly that's the good news, but his stables burned to the ground, and right now his horses have been rounded up by neighbors and taken to Ms. Joseph's place for boarding until we can get new stables constructed. I would like to secure someone quickly to start rebuilding the stables and corral. Might not be a bad idea to locate a landscaper as well. Would you mind helping me with this, Nick?"

"I'll get on it this morning. Do a little fact-finding and get back to you with estimates. It may take a couple of days for assessment before I get pricing for you to authorize, but I will do my best."

"Getting back to me with pricing to approve is not necessary. I trust your judgment. I'll have a check for you to come by and pick up at your convenience. Should it not cover the cost of the project and your time invested, I'll be happy to issue another. I appreciate your help, Nick. Oh yes, in the event I am not home when you come by, I'll ask Ms. Greenwood to give you the check."

"Mr. Statham, you are most generous. Thank you."

"Good day, Nick. Please keep me informed."

"Yes, sir. Goodbye."

———⟞∿◦⊙⟞∿◦⟝⊙⟞◦∿———

Conner was thrilled to see Vera, especially since he knew she would be departing for home that evening. He genuinely cared for her and knew she felt the same way about him. It seemed quite the dilemma that they were countries apart. Their time together had been rich. There were moments of lightheartedness and other moments of sharing the deepest parts of their hearts. He believed that this was the woman he wanted to marry, and yet how could that be in such a short time of knowing each other?

"You look good, Conner, even without eyebrows and lashes!"

"No way to mess up a handsome guy, right?"

"'Tis true. Now be still while I carefully plant a kiss on your cheek."

As she bent down, he gently reached and guided her mouth to his. "Oh, Conner, you know I'm so thankful to our heavenly Father for sparing your life. Actually, He has saved you twice in such a short time. I'm confident He has great plans for you."

"I've had some of those same thoughts this morning, plus a whole host of others about you! What shall I do when you go away?"

"Oh my, I've thought of nothing else, especially last night while we were waiting to hear word from Al. When he walked through the door this morning at four o'clock, we all pounced on him for information."

"Al is quite a guy! And that son of his, Cole, is absolutely a little prophet, wouldn't you say?"

"I've heard about his dreams and how they do seem to be visions. And, Conner, I've not been inclined to interview Al since arriving here, and now I'm to leave. I've never known a more generous and kind man than Al Statham, and to splash the details of his life in a magazine seems dreadful and almost sinful. I can tell he wants a simple life and one where he is only a vessel for God's purpose. Whatever shall I do?"

"Much wisdom is needed."

"Conner, would you pray with me? Let's hold hands and hearts together and pray for our faithful Father's wisdom and wait upon Him. He changes the course of rivers, the hearts of kings, and certainly he'll open a door that is right for both of us."

——◦◦◦◦◦◦◦◦◦——

Cole and Al sat silently eating breakfast together at the small table in the kitchen. Ms. Greenwood had asked to have the remainder of the day off. She needed to tend to many things—and her husband as well. Both had been gracious the last two weeks with much of her time required away from home. Al was thinking he should give her a week's vacation. Best not to get too spoiled.

He also had many thoughts about Conner and Vera's relationship. After all, he had introduced them! *Oh, God, please open a door for Vera to stay here in England. She has nothing but a job to go back to in America, and it is most obvious that she loves being here, and she fits into the community so nicely. Oh, Lord, please make the way smooth. And, Father, thank you for sparing Conner's life. How dreadful it might have been if you had not given Cole the vision. I have prayed that you would use us, and indeed you are answering that prayer. Thank you, precious Savior.*

Cole wanted to talk with Nya. She seemed to have a better understanding of his dreams and visions than he did. He was beginning to see that his life would never be that of a normal thirteen-year-old boy, and his emotions were not equipped to sort things out with clarity. Yes, he would ride over to Nya's today.

"Hey, Dad, I'm thinking about visiting with Nya today. Is that okay with you?"

"I don't see anything that should prohibit you from visiting today. Are you being bothered about your dreams, son?"

"How did you know? That is exactly what I've been pondering this morning."

"You and Nya have a lot in common, and I know having candid talks with Nya helps you sort through some of your feelings, but God's Word will also point you to many truths, and the Holy Spirit will reveal to you things you do not know. Just a reminder, son, to stay in your Bible."

"You have wise counsel, Dad, and I shall not neglect my Bible reading. That's a promise."

"Vera is visiting Conner at the hospital this morning. I think it would be considerate if you would arrive back home early this afternoon so we can say our goodbyes before she departs for America this evening."

"I don't want her to go, Dad!"

"Neither do I, son."

———~~◦◦ᘒᕊᕬᕊᘒ◦◦~~———

Upon hearing a soft knock at the door, Vera and Conner glanced at each other, and Vera asked, "Are we receiving guests this morning?"

"India, welcome. Please come in and visit with us. We need some sunshine, and you are just the one to deliver it!"

"I don't see any gloom in this room, but I do see two people who do not want to be separated by an ocean of water."

"Here is our wise counsel, Vera."

"India, we would welcome your input, and we have prayed this morning that God would show us clarity in our dilemma. Do you bring good tidings?"

"If it is employment you seek, Vera, here in Leeds, I cannot help you, but if you need a place to stay, Nya and I would love your company. Our house is your house. Evan rarely comes home to visit Nya, and we are always given notice when he'll arrive, so on those occasions, which are infrequent, you could stay with Al on the guest level. I know he would not object in the least."

"That is a most gracious offer, India, but of course employment would be the first order of things."

Conner spoke up quickly. "Hey, do you remember that reporter who was at the plane wreckage? I'm trying to remember his name. I'm confident Al would know."

India replied, "Yes, Al actually graced him with an interview, and I remember reading about it in the local paper of Leeds. Al would certainly know his name. Wonderful idea, Conner!"

"Truthfully, I am ready for a new chapter in my life, especially since I have no family to go back to in America. I'm free to make new choices, and choices that are led by our awesome God!"

"You have such enthusiasm, Vera. You would be a great reporter and

I'm sure a gifted writer for any company. We need to ask Al for his help. Knowing Al, he has probably already thought of this himself! He is one of the most perceptive people I've ever known."

———

Al had opened all the windows and the door, and leaned back on the sofa with nothing in mind but to rest and listen to God. He noticed the sheer drapes being blown by a gentle breeze, and suddenly an idea surfaced. Why couldn't Vera find work as a reporter and journalist right here in Leeds? He leaped up and went to his desk to search for the article that Nat had written about him. He called the number that was below Nat's name and asked to speak to Nathaniel.

"This is Nat. How may I help you?"

"Nat, this is Al Statham."

"Oh, Mr. Statham, what a surprise to hear from you. How are you?"

"We are doing great, Nat. How about yourself?"

"Good but very busy. Would love to take some time off, but we have been somewhat short-staffed, so no vacation in sight."

"Nat, the reason I am calling is to ask you to check with someone at the local paper of Leeds and inquire about an opening. I have a young friend who would like to relocate from America to England, and particularly the area of Leeds. Does this sound like something you could help us with?"

"I will try. Matter of fact, I spoke with one of the journalists in Leeds the other day, and he mentioned that since Kingston's Best was expanding so fast in Halifax, more people were moving into the surrounding areas. Hey, more people, more jobs, right? I'll give him a call right away and get back to you this afternoon, if possible."

"Nat, give this your best effort please!"

"Consider it done, Mr. Statham. We'll talk soon."

"Good day, Nat."

Al walked back to the gardens and sat on his meditation bench. He found it interesting how easy it was to praise God outside, beholding the master's grand creation. Just the other day, he watched a honeybee pollinating a fully blossomed plant. The bee would go to four or five flowers, fly off for a minute, then return to continue pollinating more blossoms. Each time he returned, he always knew where to start, where he had left off, and never landed on the same blossom twice. Only God's design could accomplish such. *Oh, God, you have made yourself abundantly visible. Thank you for giving us eyes to see your wonders. Please, Father, keep us tethered to your perfect will. Lord, this beautiful day calls for some homemade lemonade, and I believe I still remember how to make it!*

When Al entered the kitchen, he heard the phone ringing. "Could it be you, Nat? Has our Lord brought forth a miracle this fast?"

"Hello."

"Mr. Statham, it is Nat here."

"You have found an opening for my friend, haven't you, Nat?"

"As a matter of fact, I believe we have a great opportunity for her to interview for the *Leeds Daily News*. It would be filling in for someone who is going on maternity leave, and it will be available in three weeks. There is also a distinct possibility that your friend could stay on permanently if she proves to be an asset for the paper!"

"Nat, I cannot thank you enough. I am indebted to you, so please, should you ever need a favor, it is yours for the asking. My friend's name is Vera Parker, and I'll have her give you a call for the remaining details. Again, thank you so much."

"I shall look forward to hearing from Ms. Parker."

"Have a good day, Nat."

"Good day to you, sir."

—————

Vera had tears streaming from her eyes while driving back to Al's. In her heart of hearts, she knew that Conner was the man God had chosen for her, and maybe that was enough. She needed to trust her faithful God in the plan that was best. *Oh Father, help me to rest in you and live in each and every moment to the fullest. Lord, I want to live the quiet contentment of only you and, like Al, be not anxious for anything. How thankful I am that you brought godly people like Al, Conner, India, and precious Cole and Nya into my life. They are such treasures. Thank you, Jesus.*

Before she stepped out of the car, Al had opened the front door of the house. He was beaming and waving and reminded her of a young boy with such childlike expectancy. Yes, that was it! Al was a perfect example of someone with childlike faith ... so innocent, so pure, so trusting ... so apparent that he was totally a yielded vessel for God.

"Vera, come in and receive good news!"

"Things are always good with you, Al. You absolutely amaze me. Where are your sandals anyway?"

"I'm confused, right?"

"To me, you are the only person I know that is never confused. The sandals comment was my way of saying your feet seem to walk the path with Jesus so beautifully."

"I deserve no credit, Vera. Jesus has done it all. I am in awe of Him more and more each day."

"I am so blessed to have visited you and Cole and witnessed Jesus living and working in both of you. I shall never forget your kindness. These last two weeks have comforted me tremendously after the loss of my mom."

"I want you to come sit down in the kitchen and enjoy a slice of warm fruit pie with a cup of tea."

"You made this, Al?"

"Yes, I did. It is a special recipe given to me by the woman who introduced me to Jesus."

"Oh my, I know she is a wonderful person."

"Yes, she is no longer with us, but she was the best, and one day I'll share that part of my life with you, but for now, we need to make the most of the moment on your behalf!"

"I'm listening."

"It seems there is a position opening in about three weeks at the *Leeds Daily News*, and if you are interested, my friend Nat will fill you in on the details. I told him you would probably give him a call this afternoon."

# Chapter 5

Vera had set her alarm an hour early so she would not have to rush getting to work. She needed her thoughts to be organized when she tendered her resignation. Would Dana be disappointed? Surprised maybe but probably not disappointed. And then she would need to give Mr. Davidson an explanation for such an abrupt exit after the company had invested in her when she was sent to England. And of course, what she dreaded most was the fact she had no material for an article. All had been written upon her heart, never to be shared with the public.

It seemed strange waking to the sounds of the city back in her modest home. She never realized what a lousy mattress she had, and it was probably twenty years old. When she was staying at Al's place, she felt right at home and never noticed the striking opulence around her. Actually, no one took notice because of the pure motives of Al and Cole. There was absolutely no pretense. They were concerned only about matters of the heart.

Thinking about Conner brought tears to her eyes. She had called him after talking with the Personnel Department of the *Leeds Daily News* and told him about the opening that she was applying for. She had an excellent reference from Al, and the manager of personnel assured her the addition of an American employee would be well received by the small staff of their paper. Her interview was already scheduled, and she felt confident this was the Lord's direction for her life.

There were many tasks she needed to handle or at least put into motion, and the selling of her house was the top priority. She had called her uncle and told him he could have all of the furniture as well as kitchenware and appliances. He seemed very pleased, especially since Clint, his son, had just moved into an apartment and needed everything. They would pick up the furniture the day before she flew back to Leeds. Sweet Al had insisted on purchasing her plane ticket. He told her it was an investment for Conner! They had both laughed, and she hugged him for the first time. He felt like a brother to her, so caring and watchful.

She had a small inheritance of $70,000, and with the sale of the house, she would have around $200,000 along with her personal savings of perhaps $10,000. It was a start, and she knew that the investment advice of Conner and Al would grow her savings for her retirement fund. The more she thought about being a part of the lives of those back in Leeds, the more confident she became about embracing the day!

———— ∿∾◦◦⊙◦⊙◦∾∿ ————

Dana was busy getting projects organized for Vera and had placed them in neat little stacks on Vera's desk. Everything was going to get back to normal now. She desperately needed a break from the office scene. No filing had been done since Vera left, and that would be top priority upon her return, a chore everyone disliked, but it had to be done to stay organized! Over the weekend, she had begun getting excited about all the information Vera had lined up for another front-page profit maker for their magazine. The probability of another promotion was looking good!

"Sadie, hi, could you possibly do me a small favor?"

"Sure, Ms. Fulton. How can I help you?"

"I need two coffees with cream and two blueberry scones from the coffee shop downstairs. Would you be so kind? I have the correct change and will leave it on Vera's desk for you."

"I'll be right there, Ms. Fulton."

As Vera stepped in the elevator, she felt her heart pumping harder and harder. *Sweet Jesus, this is your servant to do your bidding. Please carry me in your peace, and may my conversation and conduct bring glory to you. Thank you, my loving Savior.*

She walked past her desk and knocked gently on the door of Dana's office. "Come in."

"Hey, Dana. It is good to see you. How have you been?"

"Now that you are here, I'll be fine! Hey listen, I just ordered up coffee and scones. They should be here momentarily."

"Sounds wonderful. I have not had anything to eat since noon yesterday."

"Well, where do you want to start?"

"Let's start at the beginning of my remarkable journey with the folks in Leeds."

"Vera, I am amazed. It sounds like you stayed six months and have been adopted into the family!"

"But there is more, Dana, and this part is hard for me to explain. I met someone very special. Actually, you'll remember seeing his picture in the newspaper. He was the pilot of Al and Cole's plane."

"I remember well, and what a nice-looking man! Well, congratulations, and I suppose you're going to tell me you'll be moving to England."

"That is correct. I have made arrangements to fly back in three weeks and would like to give my letter of resignation to you this morning. I want to stay at least two weeks so someone can be trained adequately without it causing a hardship for you."

"I sit here utterly amazed. It is like a fairy tale, Vera!"

"I believe it is the path God is leading me to follow, Dana."

"I guess all I can say is good luck."

"I know this is not what you were wanting to hear, but I'll work diligently through the transition and certainly don't mind working overtime without pay."

"There is so much filing to do before we bring a new person in here, so you'll have to get things up to date before we hire someone for your position. I know Mr. Davidson is going to be extremely disappointed that he assigned you to this project. I will have to take part of the blame, though, because I really pushed this whole thing!"

"Dana, there is more that I have to share with you. I need for you to know the truth about everything. I could not bring myself to interview Al. And yes, after being with him, his son, and his friends for two weeks, I witnessed enough to fill a thousand-page novel, but he desires to live simply, and I desire to honor the unspoken request of his heart. I have nothing to be published, Dana."

Sadie tapped on the door and entered with coffee and scones. "Hi, Vera! It is great to have you back!"

"Sadie, how would you like to be my assistant?"

"But Vera is your assistant, Ms. Fulton."

"Not anymore."

"Sadie, I would like for you to help Vera empty her desk and gather her belongings and escort her to her car. I need to have a conference with Mr. Davidson, and when I return, I hope to have permission for you to take Vera's place."

"Dana, I would like to speak to Mr. Davidson."

"That will not be necessary, Vera."

"Okay, then please give him this message. I have kept an account of my expenses, plus my salary for the two weeks I was in England, and I will issue a check to the company and mail it to Mr. Davidson's attention. Please share that with him, Dana."

Dana heard Vera, but she did not acknowledge her. Dana's agenda and dreams suddenly seemed like foolishness to her, and she felt small compared to Vera. She was so angry—but why? Vera lived joyfully in the moment like Al and Cole, but this type of behavior brought her little comfort; it was only a reminder that something was not right in her own heart.

After gathering her personal belongings, Vera stopped by the hot dog stand on the corner and ordered a foot-long and fries. It had been almost twenty- four hours since she had eaten, and she was famished! It felt good to sit on the little bench, peacefully eating alone and watching the people go by. Actually, she was relieved and felt liberated that she no longer had to explain herself to anyone. The whole time she was talking to Dana, she knew she was being viewed and judged in a critical way. *Thank you, Jesus, for working all of this out so perfectly. Now I shall have plenty of time to focus on the necessary things regarding my move. Oh, how I thank you, merciful Father.*

In a strange way, she already felt removed from St. Louis. The treasures of her heart were in England, and she was on a new journey to a new country to reconnect with caring friends. She felt a gentle breeze blow across her face, and thoughts of a place far away filled her heart with much joy.

Dana sat in her office reflecting on the day's events. Everyone had gone home over an hour ago, but she could not yet face going home and being alone. She had been beating herself up all afternoon for conducting herself in such a shameful way toward Vera earlier. How could she have been so haughty? When she had talked to Mr. Davidson about what happened, it seemed his disappointment was directed more at her than Vera. Who did she think she was? She knew what was at the root of all of this, but she hated to admit it—just disgusting and unbecoming pride.

# Chapter 6

Rani Greenwood was busy checking her list of seemingly endless details for Cole and Nya's going-away party. Both would be going to college in less than a week. Where had time gone? She could not believe four years had passed since she started working for Mr. Statham. They had become her family, her life, and her joy. After her husband passed away, Mr. Statham insisted she move into the guest quarters. He and Cole had comforted her through her grief and genuinely treated her like a family member. The sale of her house was handled by a friend of Mr. Statham's, and her personal belongings were moved to the guest quarters.

Mr. Statham had insisted that she call him Al after she got settled in. She had reluctantly agreed and requested that she be called by her first name, Rani.

After a few weeks, the threesome had been knitted together by God's grace, and thinking back now, she could hardly remember not being a part of the Statham family.

Cole had grown into the most extraordinary young man she had ever known. He and Nya both had old spirits, and even though they were only eighteen, their knowledge went way beyond their years, and the wisdom that the Holy Spirit had bestowed upon Cole was incomprehensible. Every day that she had lived under the same roof with this Christian family, she had marveled at Cole. He had a gift of prophesy and healing, and the humility that he walked in at such a young age astounded everyone.

The first miracle she remembered was Conner's healing. After the fire, his doctors had told him it would be weeks and perhaps months before he would fully recover, and then there would be a certain amount of scarring. That first week when Conner returned home from the hospital, Robby picked up Cole every afternoon, and the two of them assisted

Conner with meals, chores, and errands. After only one week, Conner witnessed an amazing discovery. When he returned to his doctor for new bandages, the skin on his legs was perfect! His doctor acknowledged that it was a supernatural touch. Only God could have brought about such a miraculous healing!

There were many other miracles of healing that took place in their church as well as their little community. Cole's dreams and visions were disturbing to Rani at times, especially when there was no immediate happening, but as far as she could remember, the only vision that had unduly upset Cole was the fire at Conner's place. He was never impatient or troubled. He had full reliance on his Savior, Jesus. Her life with the Stathams was always an unveiling of God's fresh revelations, and to witness such gave her a spiritual dimension and strength of faith that blessed her life beyond measure.

Vera, the young lady from America, had lived with India and Nya for a few months while getting settled in her new job, and from the very beginning of her stay, she encouraged everyone to attend church together at Valley Fellowship. Valley Fellowship was a small church with less than a hundred people attending. In less than a year, the little church grew to close to eight hundred people. To accommodate the growth, so that extra services were not required, Al gave the funds to build a church that would accommodate four thousand people. The sky was the limit with Al. He expected great miracles from God, and now the church held two services on Sunday, and the sanctuary was filled to capacity.

Al had retired from his business. After two years of working at the Halifax office, the business had more than tripled in size, and profits continued to rise as God poured out his favor on everything that Al touched. When time permitted, Al would consent to speak about his journey of witnessing God build a major international business from meager beginnings. His speaking engagements could have filled a two-year calendar, but he always placed family first. Even though Cole would travel with him to other countries on those rare occasions when he spoke, he was committed to a simple life in Leeds. He was a simple man but a man with a heart for God, so other people could rarely see things from Al's perspective; he always saw things from a heavenly perspective and walked in the peace of Jesus.

*My precious Lord, you've shared with me heaven's cup in these golden years of mine. Even in my grief of losing a husband, you've filled my life with your glorious riches. I have seen your face in so many events over the last four years and experienced restoration of body and renewal of mind. Thank you for allowing me to see your face in this earthly journey.*

———∽∾∾⌒⌒⌒⌒∾∾∽———

Nya was filled with excitement about relocating to Glasgow and her new journey of independence. She had poured hours into researching what college would be best for her to attend and at last selected the University of Glasgow in Scotland. She was drawn not only to the campus but to the city as well. It was a port city on the River Clyde and famed for its Victorian and art nouveau architecture. She had been enchanted by the theatre, music, and many museums when she toured the campus and the city. She had tried diligently to share her enthusiasm with Cole in hopes he, too, would want to attend school in Glasgow. Cole never wavered, not once. He had determined that Oxford was the only place he was being led to attend, and although he would always attentively listen to Nya regarding the benefits of them attending the same school, he just quietly disengaged from their conversation or either gently changed the subject. "So, there. That's it! We shall go our separate ways for a season."

The two of them had been inseparable for the last few years, and her heart ached each time she imagined life without her buddy, her mentor, and her very best friend. At times, she would start doubting her decision to move to Glasgow. But there was always the future to dream about, and she must have faith in God to bring Cole to her in His timing. Absolutely nothing could break the bond between them. This she knew!

The excitement of their farewell party made her as giddy as a tickled child! Ms. Rani and Ms. Vera had worked together on all the details. An extra bonus was going to be the arrival of Ms. Dana from America. It would be a surprise for Cole. He had been so fond of Ms. Dana, and Vera felt this was great timing for all of them to reconnect. Mr. Al was in agreement, too. Ms. Vera had always prayed that God would present an opportunity for Dana to accept Christ as her Savior. *Father, let it be. Ms. Vera has been instrumental in helping all of us connect with the body of Christ in our church and community. And, sweet Jesus, thank you for bringing Mr. Conner and Ms. Vera together in such a beautiful union. Their baby boy will soon be arriving, and I know he is made in your perfect image. Please keep mother and baby safe, Lord. Oh, Lord, today I give you honor and glory for all you have done. As Cole and I go our separate ways, please keep our hearts tethered to you and one another. Thank you, sweet Jesus. Oh yes, Father, one more request. In your timing, please bring Aunt India and Mr. Al together. Both of them have placed their lives on hold for the sake of Cole and me. Actually, they have spent many years promoting our lives, with little or no thought of their own personal lives. While we are away going to college, let them revel in one another. Let this be their time, sweet Jesus.*

Dana could not believe she would soon see Al, Cole, and Vera. She was in full view of Al's estate, and it was an awesome sight, actually a small palace. So this was how the rich and famous lived. There were several large white tents strategically placed on the lush green grass, and people were scurrying about with trays of food. A small orchestra and piano were clustered under a red tent, and the fabric looked to be a shiny satin with dangling crystals. As a gentle breeze blew, she witnessed all the colors of the rainbow dancing around the crystals from the sun's rays. It was the first thing that caught her eye when she stepped out of the car.

Conner had grabbed her luggage and come around to her side of the car to assist her. She felt like she was in an old world and at the same time stepping into a new world. Vera was so fortunate to have Conner. He was a gracious and gentle soul, and during their ride from the airport, he had shared many things about his life with Vera and how he adored his wife.

"Okay, Dana, we've arrived just in time for the celebration! I'll run your luggage up to the guest quarters after I deposit you in Cole's space. Your presence will be the best part of this farewell party."

"Do you really think so? I'm a little anxious."

"Cole has talked of you many times and always wanted you to visit and ride horses with him. After all, you are the one who introduced him to horses, and they are a big part of his life. He'll be thrilled that you are staying a couple of days before he departs. I know he'll have many things to share with you. We are delighted that you consented to join us!"

As Dana started through the front entrance, Cole caught her and spun her around. "I would know you anywhere. What a wonderful surprise!"

"Cole, you are such a beautiful young man. I'm not at all sure I would have recognized you. You've gone from a boy to a man in such a short time!"

"I'm assuming everyone knew you would be joining us but me! It is truly amazing that your coming to England has been such a well-kept secret! Let's see, you've had a chance to talk with Conner, but you've not yet seen my dad or Vera, right?"

"That is correct, Cole. My, what a mature young man you are, and I suppose you know you look just like your dad!"

"Yes, I've been told on many occasions that we have a strong resemblance." Squeezing her hand, Cole led her to his dad's side. "Finally, here she is Dad!"

Al took her hand, and she felt drawn to him. She stepped forward and gave him a gentle embrace, and he responded with a warm smile and a gentle hug. She seemed suspended in a dreamlike state. How could she have rejected Al all those years ago?

Vera tapped her on the shoulder. "How about a hug for the two of us?"

"That's right, there is you and the little one. How about a side hug?"

"Our only option at this point!"

"Vera, you are radiant little mother. Congratulations to you and Conner. When is your little one expected?"

"In less than a month; I'm about to pop!"

"At least the summer is not as steamy here as it is in the States!"

"True. Hey, Cole, would you make sure Dana has something cool to drink and also introduce her to our other guests and friends?"

"It is totally my pleasure. Shall we, Ms. Dana?"

———— ∞∞∞∞∞∞ ————

That night as Dana viewed a full moon from the window of her bedroom, her heart was both happy and sad. She could never remember having such melancholy feelings. Reconnecting with Al and Cole felt like a mini homecoming, and she could not understand this deep connection after so many years apart with no communication. It seemed that her heart was aglow, even though her body was beyond weariness. Perhaps it was the combination of jet lag, inadequate sleep, meeting so many people, and dealing with her own emotions regarding her past actions with Al and

Vera. She was certain of one thing, and that was her desire to reestablish a relationship with Al. She knew it the moment she saw him.

Toward the end of the party, Al and India stood together and spoke to everyone in appreciation of their presence and of the contributions that were made to Cole and Nya. There was praise and thanks expressed to everyone regarding the community's support for both children with regard to promoting Christian values. And there it was again; the word "Christian" had been brought to her attention. There had been a noticeable exchange of affection between Al and India, and just the thought of this made her resent India. India was not beautiful, but she was an exotic-looking creature with stunning eyes that seemed to look into your very soul. Dana had observed her closely throughout the events of the afternoon. India was reserved, but when she said something, everyone listened with attentiveness. Yes, she was a bit of a mystery to Dana.

In the distance, Dana heard the stirring of the horses in the stables. She eased out of her bed and looked out the large window in her bedroom. There in the moonlight, she could see a rider mount a horse and canter across the meadow toward the woods. Instantly, she thought of Cole and Nya. It was plain to see that they were in love and at such a young age.

She slipped back in bed and tried to rest in the moment. The sheets felt cool and soft to her skin, and she imagined herself living the rest of her life in a comfortable and secure place. She pushed all thoughts of having to become entangled in the corporate world again out of her head and drifted into a deep sleep.

Cole and Nya met by their favorite little stream in the woods. Nya had brought a couple of soft blankets and positioned them so they could see the beautiful full moon through the majestic arms of towering grand oaks by the stream. They reflected upon the afternoon events and shared their hearts' deepest concerns about going their separate ways in a few short days. The night was unusually cool, and Cole held Nya close until daybreak. Both knew that this time together could be the last chance for them to bear their souls to each other for some time to come. Each of them knew that these moments would be tucked away in a special place in their hearts and treasured forever. Their spirits were inseparable.

Al awoke earlier than usual and quietly took his first cup of coffee to his favorite place in the rear garden. As he looked out over the beautiful rose garden covered with the morning mist toward the stables, he noticed a light shining in the corral and saw Cole with Mystery. How he would miss having his son with him. There was no way to imagine the void that would be in his life after Cole left for Oxford. *Oh, my mighty God, You have blessed me beyond measure in all ways. Cole is your servant first, my son next, and I need your wisdom to help me keep a heavenly perspective as I totally release my boy into your care.*

Al thought about the day's events and the many people who attended the farewell celebration. Dana was an extraordinarily beautiful woman. She had matured in many ways since he last saw her in the States. He continued to detect a restless and searching spirit in her. He had noticed how she especially took note of India. He knew that Dana had deep feelings for him and hoped that God would present the opportunity for the two of them to have a heart-to-heart talk that would allow him to talk candidly about the Lord.

"Hey, Dad, you are up rather early after such a late night!"

"Guess I could say the same about you, son."

"True. Nya and I spent the night together under the stars, so I really haven't had any sleep. Guess I'll crash early tonight!"

"There are so many changes we will all be adjusting to in the next few weeks. I was in deep thought this morning about Dana. I do hope the Lord will draw her to Him and heal her heart. I can tell that she is seeking, and I know God wants to fill the hole in her heart."

"I can see the same longing in her, Dad. Isn't it strange how we actually have to let go of everything in order for God to do His work in us?"

"Yes, and it usually takes an event that is not necessarily pleasant for humans to give up control."

"You've been such a wise man throughout my life and always pointed me toward God and His ways. I'll have quite an adjustment in Oxford, Dad."

"All part of letting go and stepping out in faith each day, son, and you won't be by yourself. There will be voids in many hearts here after you leave."

"I think this passage will be a time of exploring what God has for your personal life with India. I know you care deeply for her. You've never allowed yourself to follow any of your dreams, Dad. I'm talking about the ones that God placed in your heart. You've been totally consumed with making my life the best possible, and the lives of everyone in our church and community since we moved to England. Become a kid again, Dad, and revel in the freedom of being true to your own heart. Enjoy who God created you to be and let your heart sing."

"Son, you sound like the parent giving advice!"

"I just want you to really enjoy the special person you are, Dad."

"Thanks, son. I will certainly ponder these things in my heart. I've thought about many of the things you have just shared and believe both of us should go forward in these changes and continue to abide in His peace and live in the moment knowing that God's fresh revelations will overcome any grief or hollowness that we experience being apart."

"That was well said, and I totally agree. Wonder if Ms. Dana is ready for an English breakfast."

"I don't know, but I would imagine Rani has quite a spread prepared!"

Father and son walked into the dining area where Dana was seated and chatting with Rani.

Dana smiled at both with sparkling eyes. "You two could pass for brothers!"

"God has been kind to me through the years, and I cannot believe I have a son who will be attending college this year. The years have flown since we were in America!"

"Cole, are we going to ride together today?"

"Absolutely! I need to freshen up after breakfast. Shouldn't take me more than thirty minutes, and then I'll saddle Samson and Rapha for us to ride. I had Mystery out last night, so we'll ride the geldings if Dad doesn't mind us confiscating his horses!"

"Sounds like a great plan for you two to catch up on the last four or five years. Anyway, I really need to tend to details regarding our trip to Oxford.

Conner had wanted to drive us, but Vera could possibly go into early labor, and that would add an anxious twist, so I invited Robby to ride along with us, and he is grateful for the opportunity to spend quality time with you, Cole."

A disappointed Dana said, "Al, please ride with us today. I would love to visit with you and Cole. It has been way too long."

Al disliked disappointing others, but he desired to be honest. "Sorry, Dana, I really do need some time to get organized today, but an early morning ride tomorrow would be great. Cole will be doing last-minute packing, so you and I can catch up then. Sound okay?"

"Yes, sounds perfect!" Actually, this suited Dana much better and would give her an opportunity to share her feelings with Al.

Rani had been placing serving dishes on the table. She had fresh-squeezed orange juice and full-bodied dark-roasted coffee to offer everyone. The table was such a beautiful presentation of fresh fruit, scones, homemade jams, fresh butter from a neighbor, maple syrup, and the most scrumptious French toast stacked high on two platters.

Cole placed a kiss on Rani's cheek. "How will I survive without your fabulous meals, Ms. Rani?"

"Perhaps your tummy will lure you home often."

"I'm confident you are right, devoted lady of the manor."

The meal was wonderful in every way. The conversation had been light and humorous. Dana was delighted by the comical banter between Al and Cole. Those two knew how to charm the ladies! Dana insisted on helping Rani after Al and Cole excused themselves from the table.

"Rani, you seem to fit in so well with this American family. Did you have many adjustments to make when you first moved in?"

"Not at all. I have been blessed every day from the very beginning. It is such a pleasure to serve Al and Cole and to be a part of their family. I've never known such generosity and kindness. Our entire community has been blessed abundantly since Al and Cole came to live here in Leeds, and it seems it was only yesterday."

"Yes, this is a lovely family, and I hope Al and Cole adjust quickly to being separated when Cole leaves this week."

"I do believe it would be hard if both did not have a personal relationship with our Lord. It would be very hard."

Cole walked back into the kitchen, grabbed Dana, and pulled her away from kitchen duty.

"Come, let's go to the stables. It is time to show you England's well-hidden paradise!"

"Sorry, Rani, guess I'm being hauled away!"

"Go and enjoy!"

"Oh, Cole, I am thrilled to be riding horses with you again after all these years! This place is truly a paradise, and you have the most beautiful horses. I'm so glad your dad was able to help you pursue your dream of riding horses. This was the perfect place for you to grow up!"

"Ms. Dana, it seems like it was only yesterday that we were riding horses on your family's ranch in Montana. These last four years or so have flown!"

"I'm thrilled to be here and am ashamed I waited so long to visit."

"I think everything has its season, and it is the right time for you to visit and see me off to Oxford."

"Rani and I were talking earlier about the adjustments you and your dad will have to make after you depart."

"Yes, he and I were discussing the same thing earlier this morning, and we both have the same spiritual posture. God will direct our steps separately as we totally trust Him. I know our Lord will help each of us reach and live our full potential for Him as we embrace people he brings into our lives. We will continue to make each moment count for Jesus."

Dana was silent while pondering the things Cole was expounding upon. There were things she did not understand but found herself wanting to understand.

"All right, lady of the meadow, I'm giving you Samson to ride. He is magnificent in every way, but don't fall in love with him because my dad would never let you take him to America! I shall ride Rapha. He is a great little quarter horse, light on his feet, and the smoothest canter you ever experienced!"

It had been a couple of years since Dana had ridden a horse, and Samson was without a doubt the most glorious creature she had had the privilege to ride. She would be forever spoiled!

The two raced across the meadow at full speed, and Dana felt lighthearted and even giddy. Cole, several yards ahead, motioned for her to follow him into the woods where there were creeks to jump and trails canopied with grand old oaks that sang to the soul.

Cole remembered the first time he met Nya, his one true love, and oh, how his heart ached, for honestly, he did not know how he could breathe without her!

Both had been so brave in making their plans over the last year. Each had a personal agenda neither could compromise, but both knew in their heart of hearts they would again come together, and then it would be forever. He had not realized that Rapha had come to a full stop, and Dana was staring at him.

"Oh, Cole, I'm sorry your heart hurts. I know these beautiful woodlands hold many thoughts of your life with Nya, but there will be many great times ahead for both of you, and I know your love for one another will stand the test of time."

"Yes, Ms. Dana, you are right. Our love will stand the test of time. Of that I'm confident."

"Did you want to ride to Nya's today for a little visit?"

"I think not. It will be all I can handle to bid her farewell tomorrow."

"Cole, tell me how you came to the decision to attend Oxford, and what goes through your mind when you think about being there?"

"In the beginning, I was nervous about the workload. I knew that I would be expected to write at least two essays a week, and too, there would be heated debates on many controversial subjects. I also know that God has given me special gifts, and they are to be used for His glory. Being a Christian at most any school today would be a challenge, but after much prayer, I believe God intends for me to totally focus on Him, and that means stepping out into the unfamiliar away from family and friends. Does that make sense, Ms. Dana?"

"It says that you are a brave and committed individual."

"It will be a time of new beginnings, especially for my dad. In many ways, he has never had a life of his own or even thought about pursuing personal dreams. Actually, he rarely considers himself in the equation. As long as I can remember knowing my dad, he has been a servant. I think it has been his goal in life … others first, always. My dad is one of a kind, Ms. Dana."

Dana did not understand the concept of being a servant and certainly not having a goal of being a servant. The entire philosophy of Al and Cole was totally foreign to her. She did know though that whatever they had, she wanted it!

The two spoke from their hearts as they meandered down the trails under graceful oak trees. The gentle breeze promoted a perfect day for riders and horses.

———∿∿⭕⭕⭕⭕⭕∿∿———

Nya had been uneasy and restless most of the day as she packed the essentials and a few of her treasures. Part of her heart would remain, and part would grieve for a season. Yes, she knew this passage would be quite an adjustment initially. Her dad was going to drive her to school, along with India. She could never remember being confined with her dad for more than an hour or so. It had been her aunt India's idea that he drive his daughter to college and help get her settled in. She was not opposed to it but was very uncomfortable. She did not know him, and he certainly did not know her. She wondered if they would ever really connect as father and daughter. Cole and Al's relationship was bound with unconditional love, and each always placed the other first. If only her mother had not died. She had not seen her dad in over a year, and he had declined attending the farewell party. She could not imagine riding in a car with him for over four hours. She must be still and trust … enough anxious thoughts.

She began thinking about ways she and Cole could stay connected at a distance. One thing that might help each of them was writing in a journal. It would not need to be every day but at least three times a week, and then the journals could be exchanged during holidays and summers! She needed to discuss this with Cole and make sure it would be a pleasant endeavor and not a chore. In many ways, Cole was a light in her life, and she had begun to think about life without the marvelous nature of her true love. *Oh, God, please tell me I've not made a mistake. I have prayed for over a year for your guidance, and you've shut not one door with regard to my going to school in Scotland. Help me to be brave and embrace each new day with expectancy of your fresh revelations and wisdom in sharing your love with others. Thank you, sweet Jesus.*

———∿∿⭕⭕⭕⭕⭕∿∿———

Rani had spent the afternoon in preparation for the evening meal. Salads and desserts had been prepared the early part of the afternoon, and she had set the dining room table with the finest china, crystal, and sterling. She had pressed the linen napkins and folded them her special way. She had snapped fresh beans from their small garden, candied the sweet potatoes, and turned the oven on high for the prime rib to sear. She looked forward to enjoying the wonderful aroma from the roast cooking most of the afternoon. Nya and India would be joining them, and India had wanted to bring homemade bread. She wondered how Dana and India would interact with one another since both women were smitten with Al. It should be an interesting evening.

The mansion was enchanting at dusk, especially since Al had employed an architectural friend at church to redesign the outside lighting. The vintage lamps reminded one of Venice. The standing lamps were installed at the entrance of the driveway where the security gate was manned and gracefully lit the way to the front steps. Other lamps were mounted in well-appointed places on every level of the house. There were many touches like these that Al had incorporated during the years. Everything about the grand mansion was inviting and represented friendliness and warmth. Opulence was never really seen or felt, for in every respect, this was the Lord's home, and what one sensed was a sweet spirit.

As India and Nya approached the front entrance that evening, Nya had a huge lump in her throat.

"Aunt India, with all my heart I want this to be an evening to remember. One of joy, laughter, and sharing the love of the Lord, but I must confess my heart is heavy."

"Oh, sweet girl, don't you think every precious soul here tonight will have the same feelings?"

"I had not thought of that, but I'm sure you are right. Why are we fearful of change? God never changes, yet events change constantly. We should remain steadfast in our spirit, knowing that God will not leave us or fail us. He will go before us and make our way clear. After all, He does have the best plan. Please pray for me, Aunt India. I want to be strong regarding embracing my future, knowing that Jesus will show me each step of the way."

"Oh, darling child, I shall pray for you faithfully, and we shall have telephone conversations regularly. Don't allow fear to make you anxious about the tomorrows. Remember how David handled Goliath. He not only slew him but conquered him with the Word of God, and we must do the same.

Stay in your Bible daily and commit to memory the promises of God, and when fear comes your way, speak the Word of God. Remember how our Lord battled Satan in the wilderness. He spoke the written Word, and Satan fled."

"Yes, Aunt India, indeed it is the Word of God that is our shield and defense. Thank you for reminding me."

"Okay, sweet girl, let's join everyone and revel in the moment, for we lack nothing in the grace and mercy of our Lord."

"Well said. Let's do it, Aunt India!"

After all the food was placed on the dining room table and everyone was seated, Al suggested they hold hands as he blessed the food.

Spirits were high, conversation was rich, and everyone ate until sated!

Rani could not help noticing how beautiful the women were, and Al and Cole beamed during the two hours of dining. It was the perfect intimate dinner to say farewell to Cole and Nya. Those two had eyes for only each other. Even though there was a sadness in both, there was glorious hope of coming together again.

The women were so sweet to offer help with the cleanup, but after clearing the table, Rani insisted that she could handle the rest, and they must make the most of the short time left to visit.

Rani could hear the hearty laughter from the living room. She listened intently for banter between Dana and India, but as far as she could tell, there was no conversation between the two women. She felt sorry for Dana. The young woman seemed lonely. Rani could almost feel her hurt at times. Dana was one of the most beautiful woman Rani had ever seen. Tomorrow would be a frenetic day, and Rani hoped that later tonight she would have an opportunity to talk with Dana before they retired.

*Dear Lord, if there is something I could share with Dana, please speak to me through your Holy Spirit. Help us all to walk in your peace tomorrow. There will be many goodbyes and farewells, and, oh Father, many hearts will be aching. May your will be done, precious Savior.*

---

Dana placed her riding clothes on the valet. She had not decided what she would wear for her flight back home, but it did need to be comfortable. There were so many activities jammed into the next day. Al had promised an early morning ride, and then Cole would be departing for Oxford around the same time she would be leaving for the airport. Such comings and goings. This house had been bursting with people and activities since she arrived.

Rani softly knocked on Dana's door. "Could we talk for a moment, Dana?"

"Of course, Rani, come in. Let's sit by the window over here."

"This is one of the most beautiful views of the back gardens. The moon is so bright tonight. You can see the glow on all the faces of the moonflowers below. They look like angel faces glowing!"

"You are right; they do!"

"Do you believe in angels, Dana?"

"I really don't know."

"If ever there was an earthly angel, Al Statham would be that being! I've never in all my years encountered someone with a heart like his. I've noticed for some time now that his life is not his own. He lives for others, only. Have you ever met such a man?"

"Honestly, I have not."

"You care deeply for him, don't you?"

"Does it show?"

"I cannot say for sure, but I have sensed it since I observed you the day of your arrival."

"I would love to have a chance to tell Al how I feel about him, but I can see he and India seem to have a chemistry. I think he is quite fond of India, Rani."

"Yes, you are correct. They do seem to be equally yoked in their spiritual walk."

"What are you saying?"

"They both have a personal relationship with Jesus, and this alone gives them common ground and many of the same interests. Dana, you may be attracted to Al because you desire a relationship with Jesus, and His light in Al is what draws you like a magnet!"

"Oh, Rani, you may be right! Since meeting Al, I've never been able to get him out of my mind. Literally, the first time I met him, I was so drawn to him. And then when I found out about his past, I loathed him because I felt he had betrayed me. Looking back now, I can see he was always honest, noble, and totally unselfish. How could I have held a grudge against him for his past mistakes? We've all made mistakes, right?"

"We are all sinners, and only God's grace, mercy, and forgiveness can change our wretchedness!"

"Rani, I do desire to have a relationship with this Jesus you speak about. Please help me … please, Rani."

"Child, I will be right back. I'm going to get my Bible, and we'll read some scripture together."

Rani had prayed that the Holy Spirit would lead her to perhaps present the plan of salvation to Dana, and she was praising her Savior for this glorious opportunity. *Lord, this is your work, and I am your humble servant. I ask you to guide me to the scriptures you want Dana to hear, and I ask this in the precious Name of Jesus. Amen.*

"Okay, sweetie, I'm back with my Bible, the truth! Our great God is so merciful to all of us. He finds us when we are not looking for Him, and He shows Himself when we are not asking for Him. He has known from the beginning of time every single detail of our lives, and He has wonderful plans for His children. Just the fact that you desire a relationship with Jesus is confirmation that the Holy Spirit is inviting you to have a relationship with Christ, and nothing shall separate you from God. Now, I want us to turn to Romans 9, starting with verse 31. 'What shall we say about such wonderful things as these? If God is for us, who can ever be against us? Since he did not spare even his own Son but gave him up for us all, won't he also give us everything else? Who dares accuse us whom God has chosen for his own? No one—for God himself has given us right standing with himself. Who then will condemn us? No one—for Christ Jesus died for us and was raised to life for us and he is sitting in the place of honor at God's right hand, pleading for us. Can anything ever separate us from Christ's love?'"

"Rani, are you saying that God has been drawing me to Him for years through people like Al, Vera, and even Cole?"

"All of those you mention are filled with God's Spirit, and that Spirit has been wooing you home, dear child. Let's turn to the book of John now."

"'For God loved the world so much that he gave his one and only Son, so that everyone who believes in him will not perish but have eternal life.'"

"This is speaking of Jesus dying on the cross to save us from our sins, right?"

"Exactly, child. The wages of sin is death, but Jesus willingly died on the cross as a sacrifice for our sins so we could be reconciled to God the Father. Our God is a holy God, and the only way man can come into His Presence is through the blood of Christ that was shed for us. When we accept Jesus as our Savior and Lord, God forgives us through the righteousness of His Son. Jesus is the only way, Dana."

"Oh, Rani, I need Jesus Christ in my life!"

"Come, Dana, let's kneel and pray."

Both women knelt beside the bed, and the moonlight shone so brightly that the entire room was aglow with light and love. Dana asked God to forgive her of her sins and invited Him into her heart to be Savior and Lord. Rani left her tattered old Bible with Dana and suggested she start reading the gospel of John.

# Chapter 7

## Ponderings and Reflections

**Cole:**

I find it hard to believe Christmas time is near, and I'll be going home for three weeks! I have thought many times how wonderful it will be to enjoy my family and Nya for three whole weeks! My nostrils are delighted when I think upon the smell of our horses, the hay, the lake, the forest, and the moss on the creek banks. I am grateful when I reflect on the last four months here at Oxford University. Staying in St. Stephen's House has been an interesting experience. My abode is plain and small, but for my demanding schedule, all I really need is an adequate workspace and a bed. To date, I have prepared for four debates, and our three-member team has managed to excel and win all four. There is one professor who challenges me at every turn. He does not like me and embarrasses me frequently. Most of the professors are cordial and helpful and seem to be genuinely interested in the students, but Professor Gordon has a critical way about him. I shall continue to be extra kind to him, for his personal life must be a troubled one. I have written in my journal, mostly thoughts for just Nya, at least once a week, and it will be interesting to exchange journals during the holidays! When we've talked on the phone, our conversations have centered around campus events and our courses. I want to share one dream in particular with her. It is about her aunt India. The dream is somewhat disconcerting, and I've had it several times, now.

*Dear Father, I do feel that I'm in your will here at Oxford, but I must confess there is a hollowness in my heart. I guess what I'm saying is that I've been lonely. Please carry me in your Holy Spirit and keep me focused on you and your purpose. Thank you for comforting me, and oh, Father, order my steps back home for a grand reunion with my loved ones. I really cannot think about my dad much, for it hurts my heart, especially if this dream of mine is the truth. Help us all each step of the way, and may your will be done. Amen.*

## Nya:

I love the magic that dusk brings to this place in the evening! I am so taken by the charm of Glasgow, and I know this is where I belong for this passage of my life. And oh, the breathtaking full moon over Squinty Bridge at night moves my soul to tears. I have thoroughly enjoyed my little garden flat on the cobbled lane away from the hustle and bustle, but I long for the forests, creeks, and meadows of home. I can hardly wait to see Cole, hug him, hold him, and be in his space! I want to feel his purity and smell his scent. I could inhale him forever!

*Dear Lord, reunite me to Cole and continue to give both of us your strength to remain faithful and true to one another while we are apart. May this Christmas be an experience that will be etched upon our hearts to relive many times over. Please give Robby a safe trip here and traveling mercies for the three of us as we return home. Amen.*

## Al:

I always feel close to Cole when I ride Mystery! Her spirit has been somewhat troubled by Cole's absence, and I feel drawn to ride her often and try to comfort her with kind words. Cole had a way that was unique with Mystery. She seemed to revel in his purity of spirit. When Cole first left, I wondered if she was going to grieve herself to death. I could hardly stand it when the days went into weeks, and still she continued to make circles around the stables and stare toward the house. She must have lost thirty pounds the first month. I could not bring myself to share this with Cole, as there was nothing he could have done. What a reunion the two will have in less than a week!

I have been troubled concerning the lack of connection with India. When Cole departed for college, I imagined a time when India and I would spend endless hours together getting to know one another. I had envisioned asking her to marry me this Christmas and presenting her with an engagement ring. I understand that her flying commitments are more frequent since Nya left, and Conner assures me that she is the same India we've always known, but I sense something is not right. She has pulled away in every area of our lives. I rarely see her at church, and when I do, she darts away for the next flight that is scheduled.

*Lord, I need my son. Even though he is young, he always gives me wise counsel. Please give him a word for me, dear Lord. This is the first time I've felt tethered to troubling emotions in a long time … really thought those days were gone. Robby has been such a comfort to me in Cole's absence. Please bless him, dear Father, and watch over the three of them as they make their way home. In the precious Name of Jesus, I ask these things. Amen.*

## *India:*

I really need to have a candid talk with Al, for I know he is puzzled over my recent behavior, and I am still trying to process the turn of events in my life! After taking Nya to Glasgow, Evan and I spent hours on end talking about everything in our lives. He seemed vulnerable to the point my heart ached, and I reached out to him in ways I had never opened up to another individual. Perhaps our joint vulnerability was the pathway to our present relationship. Our courtship has been a whirlwind of extremely intense encounters. He has flown to be with me wherever work took me for an overnight stay. I think what clinched our relationship was when we both took a flight together and vacationed in New Zealand. The combination of being in a paradise with no responsibilities, and being with a gentleman who loves me carried me away in abandonment. The freedom I felt those five days were like nothing I had ever experienced. Even though we had separate quarters, we spent most of our time together. He had visited New Zealand before, so I was the student and he the teacher. The entire trip was an enchanting experience of serendipity! Anyway, he was a true gentleman, and I fell in love with my sister's husband! How could this be? Oh, Lisa, what am I doing, here? My dear sister, I hope you would approve. It looks as though this caterpillar came out of its cocoon when my major responsibilities ceased with Nya. Wondering how we go forward from this point. Evan has spoken of giving our house to Robby, so Nya will not totally be disconnected from her home, the horses, the woods, and meadows. He mentioned that should she and Cole marry in the future, Al would have plenty of land for them to build a place of their own, and perhaps the gradual changes would not upset her as an abrupt one could do. Even though Evan has spent minimal time with Nya growing up, he seems to discern accurately the true nature of her.

*Oh, God, please help Nya to give her dad a chance. Help her to give Evan and me much grace in this process, for I know our union will be a shock! Please guide my steps in being honest with Al and Nya about my relationship with Evan. I covet your will and wisdom, dear Father. Amen.*

## Dana:

Work is work, but the people are God's people, and God has given me a passion to do His bidding. I have now read Rani's entire Bible and have such a thirst for God's Word daily. Whatever would I do without the power of the Holy Spirit? He leads me every step of every day, and I am amazed at the joy He fills me with.

*Oh, Lord, my cup is full every day, and I look forward to seeing what you will do with my life. It is yours in every capacity. Thank you for leading me to an awesome church last month. Already I feel close to the people. You have given me a desire to go home for Christmas and share with my family all the things you have taught me. I will forever be grateful to Rani for being obedient to you so I could come to know you. It is amazing that I had to fly halfway around the world to find you. Just that thought tickles me. You were here all the time, weren't you? How I love you, my precious Lord.*

## *Rani:*

I believe we'll have a white Christmas this year. My bones have been chilled since Thanksgiving, and already we are in single digits. This place is so beautiful with a thin blanket of white snow, and I know the kids would enjoy riding in the frosty air! There I go again, calling them kids. They are grown, and I'm sure we'll notice a significant difference in both of them after being on their own for the last few months. Just thinking of Cole cooking and washing his clothes gives me a chuckle! Not that he would mind doing these types of chores, but I'm trying to imagine what his thoughts were after eating his own cooking. He is such a delightful and appreciative lad, and I miss our conversations, especially those revelations from his dreams and visions. I've wondered if his studies consume him in such a way that the dreams have ceased. There will be much to talk about when he arrives home. Cole and Nya will get to visit with Austin during the holidays. Conner and Vera are in love with their baby boy, and he is the absolute joy of their lives. Oh, how I loved keeping him that afternoon Conner took Vera to see her doctor, and indeed, he was the best little thing … alert, bright eyed, and smiling the entire time. We need fresh joy in this house again. I just know Cole's presence here will help Al. I've sure been concerned about him these last couple of months. He is just not himself … almost like he has lost his joy. Lord knows he misses that son of his. I have thought about Dana every day and prayed that young lady would passionately serve the Lord. I was thrilled that she called me the other day and related that she was going home to visit her family for Christmas.

*Dear Lord, thank you for giving me the opportunity to witness to sweet Dana. Please give her that same opportunity with her own family. If it is in your will, dear Lord, bring Dana back here for another visit. It was a joyous time when she was here. She truly loved Al and Cole. Dear Father, protect all of our loved ones during their travels, bestow your wisdom, and carry us in your strength and joy. I give you my requests in the Name of Jesus. Amen.*

# The Christmas Season

From her bedroom window, Nya saw the car drive up to the front entrance of her little cottage. She grabbed her small suitcase and ran down the stairs and into the arms of her beloved.

"Oh, Cole, I can hardly believe I can touch you once again!"

"Are these tears I see, sweet Nya?"

"Sorry, but the river has been dammed, and I am overcome with relief! Oh, Robby, it is so good to see you, too. I have missed you both. Let us tarry no more; let's go home!"

During the journey home, there was a light banter between the three that lightened their spirits and ignited bursts of laughter. Cole shared experiences about friends on his debate team, and Nya talked about her love and delight of Glasgow's endless treasures.

"Robby, I believe Aunt India will be away until tomorrow, so I was wondering if we could go visit with Al and Rani for a couple of hours before going to the house?"

"Absolutely. That sounds like a fine idea!"

Rani was placing the finishing touches on the refreshments she had prepared for the little homecoming celebration. Al had been beside himself all day. He even mentioned that Mystery was in rare form when he rode her earlier. There was an element of excitement and great expectation in the air!

"Well, Al, what do you think? Have I forgotten any of the kids' favorite dishes?"

"Can't speak for the kids, but you have done a fine job of preparing a feast that delights my palate!"

"It seems like it was only yesterday that we were seeing these youngsters off to college!"

Al spoke softly. "To me it seems a lifetime ago, Rani."

"Oh, Al, you've had such a struggle, haven't you?"

"A huge hurdle, and I pray that God will help me cope in a more pleasing way this next year. I know my despondency has been a burden for you, Rani, and I apologize."

"Al, you never need to apologize for how your heart feels. Yes, I've been very concerned, but I'm confident God is ultimately in control. Sometimes certain passages that seem difficult and challenging are preparing us for changes in our lives. God's purposes shall prevail regardless. Try to take comfort in His sovereignty."

"Of course, you are right, Rani. Thanks for the pep talk!"

"I'm so excited! They should be here anytime now."

Cole and Nya were overjoyed when the gate opened, and Rani's arm could be seen waving from the front door entrance.

As Robby reached the house, Al appeared. He and Rani were beaming.

"Dad, oh, Dad, I'm so thankful to see you."

"And I you, son!"

"Rani, I need a big hug from you, dear lady of the manor!"

Al extended his hand. "Robby, thank you for getting our loved ones safely home. Please come in and make yourself at home. And, my dear Nya, you are a very welcomed sight!"

"It is wonderful to be home, Al. And dearest Rani, I've missed you and your warm hospitality!"

"Come, child. There is much to discuss, and we shall visit as we dine. I've tried to prepare a few of Cole's favorite dishes, and I know you'll enjoy them as well."

Cole and Nya reveled in the comforting and welcoming atmosphere of home.

———⁓⌇⌇⌇⌇⌇⁓———

Cole could hardly wait until morning's light so he could head out to the stables. He had intended to see Mystery when he arrived home, but time slipped away quickly, and then a fierce wind escorted a slick glaze of sleet, followed by several inches of snow, and Robby and Nya could not travel home. Actually, he was happy to have more time with Nya, and his dad and Robby were in rare form. He could not remember a more joyful occasion.

He could see that the stable lights had switched off, and there was a white glow of snow atop the roof and on the meadow. *Dear Father, how I've missed my home. This view from my bedroom window bathes my thirsty soul. You are painting an eastern sunrise right now just for me. Thank you for waking me up early so we could fellowship in the first moments of this new day. Father, give us your love, mercy, and joy. In the Name of Jesus. Amen.*

Halfway to the stables, Cole could hear Mystery pawing the ground and snorting. She was such a smart little mare. When he opened the side door, he could hear her banging the latch on her stall with her soft velvet nose. She knew he was there!

"Mystery, hey, girl, I'm home! Wow, I think you may have lost some weight. I guess you missed me as much as I missed you. I lost a few pounds, too! Good news, sweet girl; we're going to gain it back during the holidays."

Nya tried to slip in without a sound, but Mystery jerked her head and snorted.

"Good morning ... really tried to sneak in to observe you two love birds, but Mystery is just too smart!"

"Good morning to you, sweet Nya. I'm loving being with my two best girls!"

Nya gave a little frown. "Looks like Mystery is much thinner than she was the last time we saw her."

"I believe all three of us have had our share of grief the past four months."

"I am amazed, Cole. I would not have thought an animal would have grieved like this. Perhaps a dog but not a horse."

Cole hugged Mystery. "She has a special spirit. Don't you think she looks content with both of us here with her?"

"Actually, she looks as content as I feel. Let's go up to the loft. I know it's warmer there than down here."

"Now, Nya, are you trying to lure me into temptation?"

"Maybe just this one time."

She climbed the stairs and fell backward into a huge mound of hay. "Cole, please come up!"

"Hey, Nya, this moment takes me back to the first dream I had about you before we ever met. Remember my telling you about it?"

"How could I forget. I knew then we were destined to be together forever!"

Cole climbed to the loft, sat down on the hay beside Nya, and let out a contented sigh.

"Isn't it grand to be home, Nya?"

"Home is definitely where the heart is, and I'm always at home with you, Cole."

"We'll have to exchange journals during the holidays. I was faithful to write my most intimate thoughts and concerns on several occasions. How about you?"

"I must confess I did not write much, for I stayed busy with studies and also exploring Glasgow in the evenings with friends. Oh, Cole, it is such an enchanting place. My grades will probably suffer a bit, but I'm going to enjoy the whole campus experience. I feel as though I've been in a different world, perhaps living another's life rather than mine."

"I guess I can relate to a degree, but I've not had much time to have a social life. The debate team has to manage their time wisely. It has been a challenge to stay abreast of current events in addition to staying on top of all my courses. And as you said, indeed it seems I'm living some other life than my own."

"Was your dad faithful to write?"

"Thankfully, yes. How about India? Has she stayed in touch on a regular basis?"

"Not as much as I thought she would. In a way she has been a little aloof, which is not characteristic of Aunt India."

"You know, Nya, I believe there are changes happening in India's life. I've had the same dream three times now about her."

"We'll, let's have it. Tell me Cole."

"I first dreamt about India right after getting settled in Oxford. Then again I had the same dream a month or so later, and the third time was a few days before we journeyed home."

"Cole, what was your dream?"

"I've lost quite a few details, but I'm confident India has found the love of her life, and I believe she will share the news with us over the holidays!"

"If that were true, certainly I would have had news of such by now! She has written a couple of times and phoned at least a half dozen times."

"I'm just relating what it seems my spirit is led to believe."

"Then what you're saying is your dad is no longer part of Aunt India's life?"

"Yes, that is exactly what I'm saying and believe it to be true. I have sensed for the last couple of months that he was somewhat despondent, and I just know the lack of connection with India has been the reason behind his present state."

"Oh, Cole, this makes me very sad."

"I know the feeling. I hope to have some time to chat with Dad this morning and try to somewhat prepare him for this huge disappointment. He has loved India for quite some time, and I believe there was a time when she was close to him as well."

"I've been pumped for gladness not sadness during the holidays. Perhaps you are mistaken about all of this, Cole."

"I hope you are right, Nya. Come close. I want you in my arms. I've missed us. Being apart has taken some of the life out of me even though studies consumed me. There is no way to get away from the deep thoughts of the heart before falling asleep every night. Will we manage to get through three and a half more years?"

"I confess I've felt the same way, but I am determined!"

"We differ in that respect. I can't say any longer that I have a definite agenda about anything other than serving Christ wherever He chooses."

"Cole, stay put. I'll be right back."

Nya climbed down from the loft and found one of the soft horse blankets. She was back in Cole's arms in a flash, and she covered them both from head to toe in the soft flannel blanket.

Both of them relaxed into each other's arms and watched the sun's rays glimmer through the small loft window. The eastern sky was full of radiant pinks and silver clouds, and for the moment, all was well with their world.

"Hey, son, did you sleep in the barn last night?"

Cole had spotted his dad sitting on his favorite bench, looking out over the icy meadow and enjoying his morning coffee.

"No, actually I awoke rather early and could not wait to see Mystery! Then Nya joined me, and I left her sleeping in the loft. We are likely to be sleepyheads today since we stayed up so late last night!"

"You need to get another wrap if you're going to join me on my bench."

"Dad, I'm still a kid! You know I don't need a heavy coat."

"I suppose you're right. You never have been one to get cold. Come, let's visit while I finish up my coffee."

"I need to share something with you but don't know exactly where to start."

"What's on your mind, son?"

"Dad, I've had a recurring dream about India."

"I'm not surprised. She has totally been out of my life since you left for school."

"How do you feel about that?"

"Honestly? I feel depressed. I think part of it is because I've missed you more than life, and with India being absent, too, my heart has lost its joy."

"Oh, Dad, you know that the Lord is our joy, and as you've told me many times, He has the plan for our lives."

"Of course, I know you are right. I'll be okay. I just need to spend some time with you, son."

"I need to be with you, too, Dad. I want this Christmas season to be a glorious time of fellowship for us all. But I need to tell you about my dream so we can get through this together."

"You sound so serious."

"Things change, Dad, and sometimes it hurts initially. I do believe that India has found the love of her life. My dream was not clear as to who she has fallen in love with, but she won't be in our lives in the same capacity she has in the past. And I believe she will share what's going on in her life over the holidays."

"I believe you. I've felt very strongly over the past two months that India's feelings for me have changed."

"Dad, I know this is tough to hear, but I somewhat wanted to prepare you."

"No, actually, this is a relief. Now I can move forward because I understand. Thanks for sharing, Cole. I have always trusted the way in which the Holy Spirit reveals things to you in dreams and visions. You are a very special person, and I have missed you profoundly."

The two hugged and sat together silently until the sun lifted the fog.

———⁓⤸⤷⁓———

Rani heard the doorbell ring while she was still preparing breakfast and wondered who would be visiting so early.

Upon opening the door, she saw a radiant India. She had never witnessed such a glow. India had always been attractive in a reserved way, but today her eyes danced, and her skin glowed.

"India, Evan, what a surprise! How nice to have you visit us, and you are just in time for breakfast!"

"Rani, it is wonderful to see you, but we do not want to intrude. I really thought we might pick up Nya and visit and catch up while we ate breakfast at our house. The roads have thawed, and it is safe to travel."

"We had a late night last night, and I believe Nya is still asleep. Why don't you run upstairs and surprise her!"

"Great, I'll do just that!"

"Evan, why don't you have a seat in the kitchen, and I'll get you a cup of coffee."

"Thank you, Rani. That's a dandy idea."

Evan made himself at home in the kitchen and inhaled the rich aroma of Rani's fresh coffee. He remembered the last time he was in this kitchen, and the memory haunted him still. His rash behavior and shortsightedness had brought about immense pain in the lives of those he loved. He hardly recognized the man he was then. It all seemed like a dream about someone else. He despised the man he once was and prayed that God Almighty would continue to transform him into a new creature.

"Evan, do you take cream and sugar?"

"Oh, sorry, Rani, I think I drifted far away. Yes, please."

Rani suspected that Evan had horrible memories of this house since his wife had committed suicide on the second floor. She hardly knew what to say.

"Well, you're back soon, India. Didn't find Nya?"

"Not yet. Do you suppose she could be in the stables?"

"I would say that is a good guess!"

"Okay, then I'll grab my coat. Evan, are you okay staying and visiting with Rani and sipping on coffee?"

"Great combination, my dear. Not to concern yourself. Go find that daughter of mine!"

India hurried out the front entrance and headed to the stables. For some reason, there was an urgency in her mission. Perhaps she would find Nya alone, and this would be an opportune time to have a peaceful talk before the holiday plans prohibited one-on-one quiet time. As she entered the stables, she heard Mystery.

"Hey, girl, yes, you remember me. How could you forget? I've missed your sweet spirit."

"Aunt India! Didn't expect to see you here. Come give me a hug!"

"Hello, sweet girl, how are you?"

"I'm much better now that you are with me! Oh, how I've missed you, and we've both been so busy that communication has almost been nil!"

"Yes, and we're going to change that this next semester. I promise."

"Cole and I came out early this morning before daylight to see Mystery. I think she really grieved for Cole. Can you tell she lost weight?"

"Yes, I noticed. She has an uncanny attachment to Cole as well as a sensitive spirit. Poor little thing."

"We'll make sure she eats well these next three weeks while we're home."

"Nya, there is something I need to share with you, and perhaps now is a good time to do so when we're alone."

"Sure. What's on your mind?"

"This will be a difficult conversation for me, and I don't know where to start. Perhaps you could let me try to wade through my story before you start asking questions. Will you try?"

"I shall stay quiet until you are quite finished."

"I will start at the beginning then. When your dad and I got you settled at the beginning of the semester and left to start traveling back home, he opened up and disclosed many of his deepest hurts to me. We stopped to get dinner and talked at least three hours before heading on home. I was taken aback by the tenderness your dad revealed. For many years, both of us had been living lives that kept us from being true to our own hearts. Evan had lived with regret over your mother, and I had lived with the constant mission of getting you established as a well-educated young woman who would have every opportunity to lead a wholesome life and one led of the Holy Spirit. I felt a double weight of responsibility for you since you did not have a mother and had no relationship with your dad. I guess what I'm saying is I put my life on hold. And certainly that was my choice. I could have done otherwise, but I placed restrictions on my personal life. I could never let myself fall in love with Al, even though I knew he was in love with me, and there is not a better man in all the world. But I did fall in love, and it was with your dad. We have been seeing one another regularly since August, and I love him with all my heart. We will get married over the holidays, and we hope to have your blessings, Nya."

"I must admit I am totally stunned, maybe in shock. I cannot believe my ears!"

"I know what a surprise this must be, but I promise everything is going to be fine."

"I'm sure after I have time to digest all of this, I'll be able to further discuss, but for now, I think I am done talking."

"You are upset, aren't you, Nya?"

"I would say perhaps caught off guard and overwhelmed."

"I'll give you time, sweetie. Your dad is sitting at the kitchen table talking to Rani, so I must go rescue him. We've got so many decisions to make and need to go home. Why don't you get Robby to bring you to the house whenever you are ready. Sound like a plan?"

"Of course, I'll see you both later."

———⁓⧼⧽⁓———

Rani had prepared a feast for breakfast. It was a late meal since everyone had retired so late the night before. Robby and Al were joking and laughing, but Cole and Nya were serious. Rani tried to ask questions about school but could not get the kids to engage in the conversation. She wondered if India had shared some troubling news with Nya earlier. Oh, well, things could not always be festive.

Nya said, "Robby, what are your plans regarding going to the house?"

"I thought we might leave after helping Rani with the dishes. Sound okay?"

"You go on whenever you want. I think I'll stay with Cole for a while."

"Sure, I know you both have a lot of catching up to do. I'll come back later. Just give me a ring."

"Sounds good. Thanks, Robby."

"Cole, would you like to exercise Samson and Mystery? It would be refreshing to ride in the meadow. I think most of the ice has melted, and the snow is so beautiful in the woods. What do you say?"

"I say let's do it! You'll have to wear a pair of my warm pants over your jeans, and I'm sure I have a coat somewhere that is too small for me. Rani, do you have some warm gloves for Nya?"

"Absolutely. Nya, there are a couple of pairs in the middle drawer of my dresser; just help yourself. And I have a warm pair of boots in the closet. You'll find socks in the left dresser drawer. That should do it."

"Thank you, Rani. You are a mother to everyone. Whatever would we do without you? Actually, I'm sorry I've been so quiet, and since all of you are my family, I guess perhaps now is an excellent time to get this off my chest. Aunt India came out to the stables this morning and told me that she and my dad were getting married over the holidays. I already mentioned this to Cole, of course, and that's why we have not been our usual selves here at the table. Al, I know this comes as a shock to you, too."

"Nya, Cole shared with me earlier the dream he had about India being in love, so I was a wee bit prepared. Since I have seen very little of India since you guys left for school, I had already begun to suspect that the two of us would not continue a relationship. Please do not trouble yourself about me. You and I both know that God's plans are always better than our own."

"Oh, Al, you are always so accepting and kind. I have no idea how I would cope without all of you. Thank you all for being my family."

Robby placed his napkin in his plate and stood up. "Well, folks, this has been wonderful, but I probably need to get to the house. I'm sure there will be many changes to take place soon, and I need to know the facts. Rani, sorry to run out on you regarding kitchen duty, but I'll help next time. Thank you, dear lady, for the wonderful meal."

Nya excused herself from the table and ran to hug Robby.

"Nya, everything will be fine. Do not worry, okay? Promise me?"

"Okay. I'll call you later, Robby."

After Cole and Nya excused themselves and went upstairs, Al and Rani dropped into silence at the table.

"Rani, come, let's clean up all these dishes. Enough of this gloom. This house is the Lord's, and joy will reign. Joy and praise, for He has given us an abundance and poured out His favor!"

"Al, you are absolutely right. I believe I will accept your offer. Let's have another cup of coffee, too!"

———— ᠊ᠣᠣᡃᠣ᠊ᡉ᠊ᡉᡃᡉ᠊ᠣᠣᠣᠥᠥᠥᠥ ————

When Robby arrived home, India motioned for him as soon as he stepped out of the car. He had planned to check on the horses first, but they could wait. Conner had helped him the day before put out plenty of hay, sweet feed, and fresh water.

"Hey, Robby, could you come in the kitchen and talk with Evan and me?"

"Sure, be right there."

"How about a cup of coffee?"

"Sure. I'll have another cup."

"Did you have breakfast at Al's?"

"I did. Ms. Rani prepared a feast. She is quite a cook!"

"Robby, she is quite a lady, and we all love her like family."

"I agree."

Robby extended his hand to Evan. "How are you doing, Mr. Strickland?"

"Never better, Robby. Thanks for asking. Have a seat, please. India and I need to talk with you about a few things."

"Yes, sir."

"I know this may come as a surprise, Robby, and we do want your blessings. India and I will be married next week, the day after Christmas."

"Congratulations to you both. I wish you the very best."

"Now, Robby, there will be many changes, as you might imagine. But one thing that we want to leave the same is your continuing to live here.

As a matter of fact, I want to give you this place with one stipulation. And that would be that Nya will have a home here until she finishes college. She'll want to come home for the summers and holidays, and I would like for her room and most things in the house to be left as they are now. You can do with the place as you like after Nya graduates. I believe she would grieve if she could not return here, and I do not want to cause her any undue pain. We are also giving you the horses and feel confident that you can make a fair living from the sale of colts and stud fees. You have managed our stables beautifully and always turned a profit for us. I know we have scaled down on the number of horses that you train and manage, but you could bring about an increase easily with your expertise. We've thought about the expense of feed for the horses, and even though we will no longer pay you a salary, we will continue to provide hay and sweet feed for the horses until you realize a substantial increase in profits. Are you onboard with all of this, Robby?"

"Mr. Strickland, you and India have been more than fair, but I cannot accept this place as a gift. I will consent to pay an agreed-upon amount, though, if you, sir, could do the financing."

"Robby, that is more than fair. Consider it done. India and I are going to head into town this morning. There are several details we need to address before getting married. We hope you will stay close for the sake of Nya. I know our getting married has come as a huge surprise to her."

"Sir, I have no other place to go. This is home to me, and I will do my best to be supportive of Nya."

India grabbed her purse and smiled at Robby. "We will not be gone too long, Robby. Hopefully, Nya will be here upon our return. See you perhaps mid- afternoon."

"Yes, ma'am."

———〰️◦◦◦〰️———

"Nya, are you warm enough for this morning ride?"

"I think so. Not sure why I feel chilled to the bone."

"Should we make it a short ride?"

"No, the horses have missed us, and they do need exercise, and getting out in the open meadow gives me space to think and ponder the news of this morning."

"I can tell you are still upset, Nya. In all actuality though, you and I do sort of have our own lives now, and aren't you happy that your aunt and dad have found happiness with one another?"

"There is one thing I am sure of; it is not any fun being alone."

"Do you feel alone right now?"

"Cole, I really cannot express how I feel. Everything seems so jumbled up in my mind, and my spirit searches for peace and finds none."

"Come, let's tether the horses by the stream and have a walk in the woods. I brought a blanket in the saddlebag, so you won't be cold. Let's talk about your heartache, Nya."

They left the horses in a sunny spot. Cole wrapped the blanket around both of them, and they slowly strolled to familiar places where they had fond memories of happier times.

"Nya, I'll always be here for you. I know we seem somewhat detached because of the geographical gulf, but my spirit seems one with yours as it always has. Please take comfort in our spiritual union."

"Cole, I just feel displaced. Yes, that's the best I know how to explain it. My mom died, and I wanted my dad to comfort me, but he could not. I tried to view Aunt India as my mom, but something was missing. It may have been because she worked part-time, and of course, we lived in two different worlds. She was a professional, and I was a child needing a mother and a father but had neither. When I met you at such a tender age, you filled a great void in my life. I had no idea my life would change so dramatically when I went away to college. Plus, I viewed myself as fiercely independent, but this news of Aunt India marrying my dad has placed such a hollowness in my heart. In some respects, it feels like a betrayal. They are drawn to meet one another's needs but could not extend themselves to a small child. And then during the last four months of their relationship, I've been out of the picture with little or no communication. I'm feeling unloved, Cole."

"Come, let's go back to the stables, warm up, and talk all of this out, and I will pray with you, Nya."

Robby phoned Al to speak with Nya. He had hoped to bring her home before Mr. Strickland and India returned, but that was not the case. Al told him that the kids had not returned from riding. He had an uneasy feeling about Nya's heart, but none of this was his business. He knew Cole would do all he could to comfort Nya.

Since Mr. Strickland was visiting, Robby stayed out in the bunkhouse. It had a great little fireplace, and he was enjoying the roaring fire and a cup of hot cocoa with marshmallows. He let himself think back to a place in his heart and mind that he rarely traveled, for it was hurtful and also haunted him. Lisa had been such a fragile little gypsy. She could laugh and cry in almost the same instant. She had longed for a relationship with her husband, but Mr. Strickland was not a homebody, nor of the domestic breed, even with his daughter. It had always struck Robby as a strange union. When Mr. Strickland was away on business, the atmosphere was light and fun. There were times when he saw the very dark side of Lisa, but those times were few. She played with Nya as though she were a child herself. They all enjoyed creating their favorite dishes together in the kitchen. There was much laughter and lots of singing. The kitchen was the happiest room of the house. Come to think of it, it still was, especially with Rani living at Al's. How he wished the house could have been a happy place back then. He had tried in his own way to comfort Nya after her mom died. India also tried in her way as well. India was a professional though, and business usually came first. The airlines kept her super busy, and then she was busy buying and selling horses. She took both of her jobs seriously, and that left precious little time for Nya. Nya was a good sport though. Rarely did he see the child down or withdrawn, and especially after Al bought the Strickland estate and Cole and Nya were inseparable. He had never witnessed Nya so happy. He had to admit he felt responsible for Nya in many ways. He would pray, and God would answer. Of that he was sure.

India tapped on the door and then entered. "Robby, Nya called and has decided to stay another night at Al's. Would you mind taking some warm clothes over for her?"

"Not at all, Ms. India."

"Robby, I think that Nya is anything but happy over the news of Evan and I getting married."

"Give her some time, and give God time, too. She may feel somewhat displaced at the moment, but she will adjust."

"Yes, I suppose you are right. Well, Evan has departed to find lodging in town, and perhaps I need my own space, too. We shall leave all of this in God's hands."

"No better hands, Ms. India. As soon as you gather up Nya's things, I'll run them over to Al's. I'm sure if anyone can comfort Nya right now, it would be Cole. Please do not worry."

"I shan't, for I have my whole future ahead of me and a new life with my husband. There are still many details to handle before we are married on the twenty-sixth, so I best get focused!"

———— ᙡᨁᑅ᷁ᑅᨁᙡ ————

Cole had never seen such a vulnerable and fragile side of Nya. When they returned to the stables and settled the horses in their stalls with plenty of feed, they climbed again to the loft, and Nya curled up on the blankets that were warm from the glorious sunshine pouring in through the window.

"Nya, come close. Let me hold you while we pray."

"I don't feel like praying, Cole. Please pray for me."

"Of course. Dear Lord in heaven, you are our master, the potter, and we are the clay. Fashion us and mold us to be centered in your perfect will, dear Lord. We thank you that we have the privilege of honoring you and worshipping you, and through your Son, Jesus, we do not lose hope, nor will we contaminate our faith with fear. Right now, Father, I am asking you for your healing power for Nya. In the Name of Jesus, let her receive it now. Amen."

"Oh, Cole, how I've missed your pure spirit and wisdom. Hold me tight and never let me go, Cole."

The two were intertwined in the sun's rays until Nya dropped off to sleep.

Cole had an uneasy feeling. This was the second time today she had gone to sleep, and there was something about her that just did not seem normal. He could not put his finger on it, but Nya was not her usual independent self, and this concerned him.

He could not bring himself to leave her sleeping and go to the house, so he pulled the blanket over both of them and fell into a deep sleep.

———— ∽∽∽⌇⌇⌇⌇⌇⌇⌇⌇∼∼∼ ————

Rani could hardly wait until everyone gathered for their Christmas morning breakfast! She had a song in her heart that had to be sung, and she was sure most everyone in the house could hear her joyful singing. "Oh, what a Savior we have … babe, Lamb of God, Messiah, Redeemer, and glorious king." She wondered where this new song came from and immediately realized it was another gift from her heavenly Father. Oh, how she loved her Savior. This was going to be a glorious day … His birthday!

*Time to check my list. Let's see, table is set, candles are lit, fruit platters are on the table, homemade jams are placed about in colorful bowls, blueberry scones are in the warmer along with homemade biscuits, crispy bacon on platters covered with cloth napkins at each end of the table, pitchers of freshly squeezed orange juice, and a neatly wrapped present with red and green bows beside each place setting. Yes, that's just about it, except for the freshly brewed coffee, which will be poured after everyone is seated.*

She was beaming when Al stepped into the kitchen to get his second cup of coffee.

"Rani, you never cease to amaze me with your delicious variety of foods and pleasing presentations. The dining room table is set for only kings and queens."

"Our one and only king will be here, Al."

"But of course, this is true! Merry Christmas, Rani."

"Merry Christmas to you, Al, and God bless you."

"He has blessed me more than I ever deserved. I never feel the least bit worthy of all His gifts. Many times I am humbled to tears because of the mercy He has shown me and continues to show me."

"Al, you always pay it forward, and you know that. This community has been richly blessed because of your generous spirit."

"We can never out-give our Lord, Rani."

"I agree."

"Now, tell me once again, who will be joining us for breakfast this morning?"

"Conner, Vera, Austin, and Robby, a total of eight! Matter of fact, they should be arriving any time now."

"Our dearest friends will be celebrating our Lord's birthday with us. How blessed we are, Rani. By the way, what's in the beautifully wrapped gifts on the dining room table?"

"You don't mind spoiling your surprise?"

"Not at all. I'm like a child at Christmastime, just can't wait!"

"I've been working on the gifts since the kids left for college. I knitted scarves for everyone, even little Austin."

"That is a wonderful gift for us all … tis the season for such! You are too good to all of us, Rani. I cannot imagine life without you in our lives. I'm sure I don't thank you enough for all you do, but certainly you must know how much we appreciate you and love you."

"Al, I know you love me, and I adore being part of your family. My life could not be any better. God gave me a desire to cook, and creating meals for you and Cole and our guests is my heart's desire."

"I believe I hear voices at the front entrance. I'll get the door, and you bring the coffee!"

# *Chapter 8*

## *Valentine's Day, 2012*

As Nya struggled to drift off to sleep, all the day's events swirled around and around in her head like a record stuck on repeat. She had tried her best to enjoy her dad and Aunt India's visit. It was kind of them to try to fill her day with special gifts and experiences on Valentine's Day. They were full of joy and hope of a great future in New Zealand. Her dad had purchased a home in New Zealand over the Christmas holidays and surprised Aunt India with the news on their wedding day. In some ways, her family felt like strangers to her. Listening to their conversations over dinner was like being in the company of strangers. Yes, that is exactly what it felt like. Since learning of their marriage before Christmas, she had felt an odd disconnect. Even with Cole's tenderness and concern, she experienced somewhat of a disconnect. Her assignments at school seemed difficult, and her social life had dropped to zero.

*My dear, sweet Jesus, I know you desire that I be fully whole in my being ... spirit, soul, and body. Right now I ask for good health and your love. Whatever is wrong, please make things right. You, oh Lord, are my light. I only know the way when you light my path. Lord, I beg you to manifest your healing in my being. There is none other than you. In the Name of Jesus, let it be. Amen.*

As she crossed over and gradually slipped into a deep slumber, she could see and feel the blood of Jesus cascading, and then ...

---

Cole awakened in a panic. He had dreamt of Nya running from him and being lost to him. She was running away from him, and the distance was not clear because of a fog—or was it a moving and turbulent hazy wind that separated them? His thoughts were unclear, but in his spirit he knew she was in a crisis and needed immediate help. After ringing Nya's phone and getting no response, he immediately called his dad.

Al finally answered the phone. "Hello."

"Dad, something is wrong with Nya. I had a frightening dream, and I need your help."

"Should I call the campus security, son?"

"Yes—and hurry."

"Okay, somewhere in my desk I have the campus directory. I'll get back with you as soon as I have more information."

———∿∿●◖◗●◖◗●∿∿———

After calling security, Al sat with his Bible in his lap, looking over passages in the Psalms and pleading the blood of Jesus over Nya. He knew from Cole's tone that the dream he had could mean they would embrace a crisis that only their Lord and Savior could overcome for them. He thought back on all the dreams God had given Cole and thanked the Lord for His faithfulness and victories, claiming yet another victory for his Lord.

In less than thirty minutes, a gentleman from campus security called Al and reported that there was no answer at Nya's little cottage, so after much pounding on the door, it was opened by force. Nya could not be awakened, so the medics were notified, and she was en route to the hospital.

Al calmed himself before calling Cole. "Son, Nya will be arriving at the hospital soon, where she will get the help she needs. Apparently, she is some type of coma."

"I knew it, Dad. Help me. Get me to her as soon as you can."

"Listen, son. Let's not jump to conclusions. Our Lord is in control. We all need to embrace Nya and pray for God's wisdom. I'll call Robby and ask him to come with me. We'll pick you up and drive to Nya. This is all in God's timing. He is in the midst of this storm with us and will go with

115

us each step of the way. While we are en route, you give India a call. Nya needs our prayers and our presence."

"Okay, Dad. Hurry but be safe. I love you so much."

"You got it. I love you too, son."

—⁓∘◦⊶⊙⊶◦∘⁓—

Nya was not conscious during the ambulance ride, nor when she arrived at the hospital. The x-rays and scans revealed some bleeding in the left side of her brain. Al had given the emergency room doctor all the information he had regarding numbers for India and mentioned that Nya's aunt and dad could be in flight to New Zealand. The doctor said surgery would likely be required and that her parents needed to give their consent. Al told the ER doctor that close friends were en route.

Cole was finding it impossible to stay calm. His dad should have already picked him up, and he knew time was critical.

He and Nya had exchanged journals during Christmas, and tonight was the first time he had thumbed through hers. He noticed in her writings that her heart was heavy at times, which in their telephone conversations he had not picked up on. He knew her emotions ran too deep to adequately express in her journal, and if she had, it would have probably ripped his soul apart. He could only be okay if she was okay. They had always been linked in their souls.

He saw the lights from his dad's car in the parking area. Running out the door with a small overnight bag, he leaped into the car.

"Oh, Dad, thanks for coming. You too, Robby! We must hurry on our journey, stopping for nothing, for I feel it is imperative for me to get to Nya! Do you have an update on her condition?"

"Yes, son, we do. It is not good, though. Nya will probably require surgery because the left side of her brain is bleeding. And as far as we know, the doctors have not been able to talk with Evan or India for consent."

"That's good, Dad. I just need to touch her, and I know God will heal her through the powerful Name of Jesus."

The surgical staff was prepared to do surgery as soon as consent was given. Nya was still unconscious. She was on oxygen, but no drugs had been administered. Her vital signs were good; no drop in blood pressure and no fever.

The neurosurgeon felt strongly that waiting would put more pressure on the brain, but he did not want to disregard hospital policy.

Dr. Foster decided to have another scan done on Nya, just to make sure they were not placing her in grave danger by waiting. He also decided to give the administrator of the medical center a call to discuss the hospital's liability should he need to do surgery without a consent. She was such a young girl with her whole life ahead of her, and he could not stand by and do nothing if her life was at risk.

The administrator, of course, advised that things needed to stay in a holding pattern until a parent or guardian could be reached. Dr. Foster had surmised as much because of malpractice suits.

One of the nurses approached Dr. Foster with a message to give the radiologist a call regarding Nya's last scan.

"Hello. Dr. Foster here. Do you have an update on the Strickland girl's condition?"

"Yes, we are seeing more bleeding now. We thought it would have slowed down or stopped, but perhaps you need to take a look at the scan in order to make a decision regarding surgery."

"I'll be right there."

After viewing the scan with the radiologist, there was only one thing to do, and that was relieve the pressure and try to stop the bleeding. The scans were done four hours apart, and they simply could wait no longer. He knew all of this would be reviewed after the fact, and he could even lose his license, but none of that mattered compared to saving a life.

As he was walking back to Nya's, room there was a commotion at the nurse's station. Three men were insisting they be able to see Miss Strickland.

"I'm Dr. Foster, Miss Strickland's surgeon, and we are taking her to emergency surgery right away. Feel free to wait in the waiting room on the third floor, and I'll talk with you after the surgery."

Cole grabbed Dr. Foster's hand and kneeled down, begging to see Nya before surgery.

"She is my best friend in all this world, and I know if I can touch her, she will awake from this coma!"

"What's your name?"

"Sir, my name is Cole, and Nya and I have been together for the last several years until we parted to attend college. Please, sir, just let me hold her hand for only a moment?"

"Come with me now but only for a moment. Time is not on our side."

As Cole entered the room, he felt dizzy and a bit disoriented. He went straight to the bed and cupped Nya's hand in both of his, pressing her soft skin to his lips. She seemed far away in her spirit, but he knew the Spirit of God would revive, for that is what His Word says.

He placed his hand on the left side of her head and said, "Be ye healed in the Name of Jesus."

Dr. Foster looked both stricken and perplexed. "Son, that's enough now. We have to get your friend to surgery. You need to wait on third."

Cole bent down to kiss Nya, and when his lips touched hers, she opened her eyes wide.

"Where are we, Cole?"

"Oh, Nya, you are in the hospital, but we shall soon take you home. You are going to be fine."

"Young lady, I am Dr. Foster, and we've been monitoring some bleeding in the left side of your brain. The last scan results revealed that surgery is needed to relieve the pressure and try to stop the bleeding."

"But I feel perfect. Why should I have surgery?"

Cole finally got his wits about him and asked about another scan since Nya seemed normal.

"You see, Dr. Foster, we believe God is still in the business of miracles today."

"I agree," Nya said. "And should the scan reveal the same results, I will consent to your doing surgery to relieve the pressure."

"Okay, Miss Strickland, let's get you back to the x-ray department— and quickly!"

"Cole, please come with me. Don't leave me."

"I'm right here and going nowhere, Nya."

———⁓⁓⌒⌒⌒⌒⁓⁓———

Al and Robby had gone up to the third-floor waiting room. It had been a whirlwind night of urgency and fast driving. Al had never driven so fast in all his life, not even as a wild and crazy teenager. He would do anything for his son though.

"Robby, I guess my driving was a little crazy. Sorry to drag you out of bed and then scare you to death."

"It's all good, Al. I have not felt one ounce of fear. I've always had total confidence in your decisions and abilities. You are a true man of God, and I know He goes before you."

"You know, Robby, I've had a check in my spirit since Nya was home for the holidays. I know the news of her dad getting married to India hit her hard, but that was not all of it. She was just not her usual carefree self. Did you sense the same?"

"Now that you mention it, I agree with you. She was unusually quiet and somewhat withdrawn. Perhaps her brain was not functioning normally."

"We know speculation will get us nowhere, so let's rely on our great God to heal our girl. Robby, let's pray together now."

"Okay, Al."

"Father, you, oh Lord, are the great I am, and there is no other like you. We have faith to believe you can heal Nya, even without surgery, dear Lord. We believe that since you gave Cole a vision of Nya's condition tonight, you will also heal our girl. Father, your scriptures declare that you were amazed at the faith of many who were healed. We beg you to give us that same measure of faith so you will be amazed at our faith in you, for we love you with all of our hearts. Lord, receive our petitions in the powerful Name of Jesus. Amen."

Robby had tears running down both cheeks and a huge lump in his throat. Al's praying always brought him to his knees.

When Al looked up, he thought he was dreaming. Cole and Nya were walking through the waiting room doors.

"Come here, kids. Let's have a group hug and give thanks to our good Lord above!"

———— ∽◦◦ᘓᕐᘍᕐᘓ◦◦∽ ————

Nya directed Al to a charming place where they could eat a good breakfast before the journey home. Nya and Cole cuddled close on one side of the booth, with Al and Robby across from them. Nya's eyes were bright, and her smile was radiant. Indeed, she seemed to be back to her normal self!

"I want to give our great God thanks for my healing, and I want you three to know that the happiness each of us seek is truly found only in loving and being loved by the one true God. I know my whole life has been transformed with God's touch of healing. He has healed my heart, my mind, my body, and my spirit. Now, this is probably going to come as a surprise, and I hope you will be patient with me. I want to go home. We could gather my belongings from the cottage and run by the admissions office and then be on our way. I need to withdraw from my classes. After getting settled in at home, I will enroll in online classes. There is much unraveling the Lord needs to do in my soul, and there is no better place to start than home."

Cole took her hand and said, "We support you totally in whatever direction you know the Lord is leading you."

"I have a very special request of you, Al. You know you have always felt like family to me, just as you have, too, Robby. I would like to live at your house, Al, on the second floor in the small room beside Rani's. I know Robby needs to go forward in making a living and having the freedom to redesign the house to fit his needs, but besides that, I want to make peace with my past where my mother and I played together, danced together, and slept together. Al, your house is a happy house now, and that's the way I want to think upon my memories with Mom. Am I making sense or just babbling?"

Al reached across and took her hand. "You are making perfect sense, Nya. And yes, you are more than welcome to make your home with Rani and me. I am humbled and honored that you desire to stay with us."

Nya looked at Cole. "Are you okay with my leaving college and living back home?"

"Nya, I am more than okay; I am elated, for I know without a doubt you will be truly happy."

He drew her to him. Both had tears of joy and hearts full of joy.

"Cole, God saved my life through *you!* Do you find all this hard to believe?"

"It really seems fairly natural. Miracle on top of miracle, so I'm not surprised. He has been doing this since the beginning of time, I believe!"

At that statement, everyone laughed and laughed. It would be a memorable breakfast for sure!

# Chapter 9

Life had been simple and yet very rich the last few months. Nya adored living with Rani and Al. Al had taken great care to cover every detail to ensure she felt this was her home. And Rani had truly been a mom to her since she arrived in February. Her room was well lit with windows from floor to ceiling, and the window dressings were light blue silk, and just recently with the change of weather, the curtains flowed and rippled with the breeze. Rani had bought her a sewing machine, which was set up by the largest window. The two of them had had several days of shopping for material and patterns, and the clothes Rani had taught her to make were so beautiful. She was getting excited thinking about how Cole would react to seeing her in casual, flowing dresses when he returned for the summer. She had missed him profoundly, but they spoke on the phone regularly, and she wrote him long letters that she felt would be of interest to him regarding the changes that Al had implemented in new and unique ways of breeding and selling horses. Al had solicited Conner's help and given Robby control of training. The three were in perfect concert. She knew Cole would be pleased to see his dad passionately involved in such an exciting adventure!

When she first arrived home, she had stayed at the house with Robby for a few days. There were of course many decisions to make regarding what to take to Al's and what to leave or discard. When she was finally ready to move, Robby packed her things in the truck, and she said goodbye to her home.

When she arrived at Al's, he and Rani were standing at the front door with gracious smiles and arms held open to embrace her. Rani was absolutely radiant and full of her sweet self. She asked Robby to place the suitcases at the front entrance so things could gradually be placed in their proper place. She escorted Nya to the second level where Nya would share the room beside hers. What a surprise! She and Al had been extremely busy tending to every detail imaginable in such a short time. The room was exquisite. The walls were a whitewash with an empire chandelier in the center, and the crystals were the colors of the rainbow. The curtains were of a delicate light blue, and the bedding was a blend of silk and satin in a slightly darker tone with a lace dust ruffle. At the foot of the bed was a beautiful chest made of rosewood. The dresser, headboard, and nightstands were made of rosewood as well, and the pink crystals brought the delightful wood to life. There was a huge, white, circular area rug at the end of the bed and two smaller circular rugs on each side of the bed; sweet warmth atop the pure white marble floor. The room was perfect, and adjoining it was the perfect ladies' room with a walk-in closet, beautiful dressing table, and a double window with the most exquisite pieces of stained-glass installed. The colors in the glass were clear, white, and blue green. The windows opened from the center. It was absolutely magnificent. Her quarters were enchanting and so inviting.

When she and Rani were making her dresses, she would sometimes stay in her bedroom all day. The outside light coming through the large windows created an atmosphere of sheer freedom, and she could look out and see the sun rising beyond the meadow and enjoy the horses frolicking in the grass. It was her little piece of heaven!

She had cherished all the late-night talks with Rani. God gave Rani the most tender nurturing qualities of anyone she had ever been around, and she adored her. She imagined that she would have loved her mother as she loved Rani, if her mother were still alive. Rani put her heart and soul into everyone she touched and everything she touched; she was a lover of God and His creation.

---

Al was on his favorite bench with his morning coffee. "Oh, what a special time this is."

He had a plan that had been stirring around in his head for a few weeks now. Having Nya living with them had helped him to see the future would be changing soon, especially for Cole. Although the two were young in age, both had old spirits and wise souls. He had called the architect who had done additions on the house and asked to meet with him regarding building another house on the adjoining property he had recently purchased. It actually added two hundred more acres to the present property. He and Angelo had met several times over the last couple of weeks and determined where the house would be built, as well as additional stables.

Conner had helped him acquire a dozen or so mares and one stallion so they could enjoy ranching together. Most of the mares were purchased within a few hundred miles of their place, but the stallion had been purchased from Saudi Arabia. The bloodline of the stallion was matchless. Conner had flown over to make an offer on him, and he stayed until he could arrange to travel back with the stallion. The mares were presently in the stables with Sampson, Rapha, and Mystery, and the stallion was at Conner's. Later when the house and stables were finished, the stallion would be moved. He was the most magnificent creature Al had ever seen. There was no way to describe him. He was such a shiny black that he looked bluish silver. One just had to see him to believe the spectacular beauty—absolutely splendid! The stallion had never been ridden, and Robby was going to break him gently and train him. Between Robby and Conner, Al felt that his ranch would be unique, and people from other countries would be drawn to purchase the colts and fillies raised on his ranch.

His mind had drifted back to Dana the last couple of days. Rani stayed in touch with her and said she was busy with her profession and also busy volunteering in different outreach ministries at her church. Al smiled when he thought about Dana serving the Lord. "There is no one like our awesome God when it comes to transforming weak and lost humans!"

*Dear Father, when I look around at how you've enlarged my territory, and behold all your blessings, I can hardly believe it is me, Al Statham, who you have blessed beyond all imagination. Lord, my most valuable blessings are my son, Rani, and Nya. Rani has become the mother to me that Mayme once was. It seems unreal that you blessed me with a mother in America and another mother in England. You have met my needs with a beautiful family and loyal and loving friends. What more could a man want? Thank you, my sweet Savior, for drawing me to you. You loved me before I knew you, and you knew me before I knew you. That is what makes you, my sovereign God, so awesome! I love you, Jesus.*

———— ∿∾᧧ᘏᘓᘔᘏ᧧∾∿ ————

Cole was thinking about Professor Gordon's reaction to their meeting. He tried to put himself in Professor Gordon's shoes, so he might anticipate the response his professor would have after listening to his dream.

Cole never questioned his dreams. He knew that God intended his dreams and visions for His glory. The dreams of Conner and Nya were by far the most urgent dreams he had had. He had been praying about the right timing to speak with Professor Gordon, and it seemed that this week his spirit was being summoned to take action. He felt the finger of God was on this meeting.

Class had been dismissed. Professor Gordon sat at his desk, and Cole continued to linger in the classroom.

"Cole, is there something I can do for you?"

"Yes, sir. If you have a moment, I would like to talk with you in private."

"A moment is about all I have."

"Sir, shall I close the door and pull up a chair?"

"Let's make this quick; I have critical issues pending."

"Yes, sir, I know that your heart is heavy regarding your son."

"How do you know about my personal life? Where did you get your information? Have you been meddling in my affairs, young man, or spying on me?"

"No, sir. I could never do that. Let me explain, Professor Gordon. Since I was a young boy, the Lord has given me dreams and visions, some of which saved people's lives. I had a dream about your son's eyes. I believe he has very little eyesight, and you are solely responsible for his care and have become discouraged and concerned about your finances as well. I realize I'm being extremely forward, but I only know how to approach this with the entire truth as it is revealed to me. In my dream, your son's vision is restored. This may be hard for you to believe, but it shall come true, sir."

"I don't know what to say. I don't even know what I think. You have to know I want to believe you. You are correct about Graham's eyes, and we have lost hope and exhausted our funds. I have been tormented this entire year just trying to make ends meet for us. Our place is very modest but expensive since it is near the college."

"Professor Gordon, my dad has always given his time and money to worthy causes, and after I had my dream about Graham, I talked with him, and he volunteered to do some networking with friends in America regarding eye surgeons. He called me the other night and told me to have you call him. I received a letter in the mail yesterday, and enclosed was this envelope addressed to you."

Professor Gordon slowly opened the letter. Before he could read it, a check slipped out and landed on the desk. He gasped when he looked down.

"I could never accept this, Cole!"

"It is for your son. My Father in heaven desires you graciously accept it, and my dad is a very wealthy man and loves to bless others. He wants your son to be healed and your soul to also be healed."

"I don't know what to say."

"Go home and share with Graham that he shall see very soon!"

"Cole, I've been so unkind to you. I have singled you out, and I don't know why."

"I've prayed for you all year, Professor Gordon. I knew in my heart God's purpose would be served."

"Cole, you are a remarkable young man. I am so ashamed of myself. Can you please forgive me, son?"

"There is nothing to forgive. Let's give God the glory, and you give my dad a call so you and your son can start on this wonderful mission and give our great God all the credit!"

———❧◦❧◦❧◦❧———

Rani and Nya were placing the finishing touches on two of Nya's dresses. They were sewing lace and pearls by hand around the necklines and sleeves. Both dresses were made from soft silk fabrics. The light green was empire style, and the light pink was made to fall below the waist with a beautiful sash.

"I'm going to get us some more tea, Nya. Peach or mango?"

"I think I'll have the mango, Rani. And would you mind bringing us a slice of Al's fruit pie? He amazes me when he gets in the kitchen. I have to admit his fruit pies just cannot be topped!"

"I agree. Okay, when I return, let's chat about Dana coming to visit this summer."

Nya remembered Dana as being somewhat sad when she visited. Last summer seemed such a long time ago. So much had changed in her life since then. Actually, she felt like a different person.

"Refreshments are served."

"Thanks, Rani. You are such a dear."

"Well, I did talk with Dana. I asked her to pray about visiting us this summer while Cole was home. She is good at reading between the lines and asked me how Al felt about her visiting. And of course, I had to tell her that he did not yet know of my invitation. I will need to talk with Al about this, for Dana will not consider coming without his consent."

"I would feel exactly the same way, Rani."

"Since I've stayed in touch with Dana, I really felt at liberty to extend an invitation without Al's permission, but I was wrong. I will talk with him soon."

"Dana is a horse woman, right?"

"Well, she grew up on a ranch in Montana, so I would think she has plenty of experience."

"That's good because Al intends for his ranch to have the finest horses money can buy, and that will take experienced handlers and trainers. Dana could possibly have experience she could share with Al that would be vital!"

"Nya, that would be a great way to approach Al regarding Dana visiting us, don't you think?"

"Indeed I do. Dana would lend expertise in western riding, and that would be appealing for Americans desiring to visit our ranch! Aside from the professional view, I would love to see Al get his joy back and the sparkle in his eyes, and Dana may be just our gal!"

"Let us pray together about this. I know the Lord will go before us and lead accordingly. He always does."

Cole could hardly believe he would be seeing Nya in a matter of minutes. He and his dad had talked nonstop on his trip home. It was just the two of them, and he was thankful they could have one-on-one time with each other. He could not remember when they had talked so freely about so many issues.

His dad had been excited about the new mares and stallion he had recently purchased. He talked on and on about the concept of having a ranch that would bring serious ranchers and horse breeders to their place. He also expressed how Nya had been a gracious addition to their family. Both found it interesting and somewhat sad that her dad and India had not visited, nor had they kept in touch with Nya on a regular basis. This broke Cole's heart, for he knew how much family meant to Nya.

The car was slowing down to make the turn into the long driveway, and Cole put his window down so he could smell the country air. The honeysuckle reminded him of the woods bordering the meadow and the scent of Nya perched on a saddle freshly rubbed down with saddle soap. The combination of smells transported his emotions to a state of abandon and spiritual freedom. This was a different world. It was his paradise. It was his home.

He drew in a breath. "Dad, I couldn't be happier. How I've missed our place and my precious family."

"We have two and a half months to ride horses, enjoy Rani's feasts, enjoy the fellowship of our community, and pray for discernment regarding God's direction for your life—and of course Nya's."

Nya and Rani could not wait inside. Both had been standing at the front entrance to the house for at least thirty minutes. Nya's heart fluttered like a butterfly when she saw the car. Rani was excited, too. She loved having this sweet family under one roof. There simply was nothing quite like it. How she loved them all!

Cole leaped out of the car. Nya flew into his arms, and Al and Rani shed a few tears.

Finally, Cole released Nya and held her at arm's length, admiring her long, flowing dress.

"How do you like?"

"I really like. You are quite the woman, Nya!"

"Rani and I designed it, and I made it on my new sewing machine. A little uncharacteristic of me, wouldn't you say?"

"You've always been creative in many ways, so I'm not at all surprised. You are beautiful, Nya."

Al reached for Cole's luggage, walked past the two, and he and Rani went inside so the lovebirds could have their time together.

———⁓⁓⁓⁓⁓⁓———

The day seemed to end all too quickly. Cole and Nya had saddled Samson and Mystery and spent hours together exploring the newly acquired land. The new ranch house already had a roof, and the stables were almost finished. The stables were elaborate, and the corral was beautiful and unusually large. The fence was higher than normal, so Cole speculated that this would be the home of the stallion. Inside the stables on the second level were living quarters for a full- time trainer. His dad had thought of everything. Cole was reminded of how this dream started. If it had not been for Ms. Dana introducing him to horses and taking him to her family's ranch, what he was witnessing might never have been. God's purpose comes to light through His people being connected. The house was a sprawling ranch style. The front area of the house had mostly glass panels. The great room, dining room, and kitchen were housed within the glass panels. It was in the shape of a semicircle with a large courtyard in the back. Actually, the courtyard could be seen from the front entrance because of the glass enclosure. A long wing extended from each end of the glassed area. Both wings were the same—three bedrooms and baths and a sunroom and patio area at the end of each. Each wing had skylights as well as large windows for optimal lighting. The whole place was designed to bring the outside in. The burnt-orange clay roof had been completed, but there was no siding on the house yet. Cole hoped it would be a stone house rather than brick. He knew whatever his dad had in mind would be perfect.

The day was full of sharing personal experiences and hopes and dreams. Nya had mentioned that she and Rani wanted to invite Dana to visit during the summer. Cole wanted to talk with his dad about extending an invitation soon. Nya mentioned that she had gotten a telephone call from her dad earlier in the day, and he and India had extended an invitation for her to come visit them in New Zealand. She was somewhat conflicted about leaving Cole, and both agreed to pray about it, knowing God would direct her.

After dinner, everyone strolled the gardens and beheld an incredible sunset of oranges, purples, and pinks. It had been a glorious day, and all hearts were grateful. When Al and Rani retired for the night, Cole and Nya raided the refrigerator and consumed the last two slices of fruit pie and shared a glass of milk at the kitchen table.

Cole quietly asked, "Have you thought any more about your dad's invitation to visit him in New Zealand?"

"Actually, I've thought of little else. If you were going with me, I would be on a plane tomorrow, but I could never take you away from your dad. After all, you've been away for nine months except for the brief Christmas break."

"I've had the same thoughts, Nya."

"Well, I say you and I make the most of the first part of the summer. Perhaps check with Dana and see about a visit from her if your dad is amenable, and beyond that, just pray that the Holy Spirit will guide me regarding a trip abroad. New Zealand is over ten thousand miles away, and right now I want you to be no more than ten steps away from me!"

Cole stood up, pulled Nya to him, and kissed her deeply. They clung to one another as though thoughts of the future were threatening in a strange way.

"I would love to go to the barn for a while, maybe have a ride in the moonlight, but all of a sudden I'm feeling extremely fatigued. Could be the long trip today. Hope you are not disappointed, but I'm ready to get some sleep. How about you?"

Nya agreed. "Go ahead, Cole. I'm going back out to the gardens to ponder and pray. I need time alone with God this evening."

He pressed his lips gently on her mouth and bid her good night.

Before going upstairs, he headed to his dad's room. He could see light coming from under the door, so he knocked gently before opening.

"What's up, Cole?"

"I've been thinking about Ms. Dana and her expertise regarding horses.

What do you say we invite her to come for a visit? It could be professional and pleasure. I've thought about her often since India married Nya's dad."

"Interesting that you mention this now, because only yesterday I was thinking the same thing. Let's do it!"

"Oh, Dad, that's great. Let's give her a call tomorrow, okay?"

"Sounds like a plan. Anything else on your mind, son?"

"Quite a bit, but I am too tired to share. Let's talk tomorrow."

"Night, son."

"See you in the morning, Dad."

Cole loved being in his room. Actually, he loved being under the same roof with his dad and Nya. Since Nya mentioned going to New Zealand, he had not been able to totally surrender to the peace of Jesus. And there were other disturbances in his spirit as well. He could not seem to focus. Even though he was totally exhausted from the day, his mind did not want sleep to overtake.

*Oh, Lord, I only see in part, and even when I have dreams and visions, there is no way to clearly discern. I understand that you are the lamp of my path and that things are revealed only when it serves your purpose, and I must remain calm and confident in you. I do understand, Lord, that the gifts you have given me are only to be used when you direct me, and I am beginning to see more and more that my life is not mine but yours. Please give me peace regarding Nya's visit to see her dad, and give me clarification regarding my connection with Professor Gordon and his son, Graham. I continue to feel a definite pulling to both. Until the time comes for you to reveal, please carry me in your peace, precious Lord.*

---

Rani could not imagine who would be ringing the front doorbell before breakfast.

She swung the door open and smiled at strangers. "Hello. May I help you?"

"We came by uninvited, and for that we apologize. I am Mr. Gordon, and this is my son, Graham. Cole is one of my students."

"Say no more. Please come in. Matter of fact, we would love to have you join us for breakfast. My name is Rani."

"Very nice to meet you, but we could not impose, and we only came by to thank Mr. Statham for all of his help and give him an update on Graham's condition."

"Please have a seat here in the living room. The family will be in shortly, and you'll be able to visit with Mr. Statham and Cole as well."

"Thank you."

"Please tell me what you like in your coffee or tea?"

Graham said, "Would you have any hot chocolate by chance?"

"Absolutely. And you, Mr. Gordon?"

"Black coffee would be wonderful!"

Cole entered the living room, and to his surprise, Mr. Gordon abruptly stood and greeted him.

"Cole, I know this is quite a surprise. It is good to see you."

"It is great to see you, Professor Gordon. And I assume this is Graham with you?"

"Yes, Graham, this is Cole."

"Cole, we could never thank you and your dad adequately for all you've done for us."

"We are so pleased to have you visit. Please sit back down. I'm sure Rani has already invited you to stay for breakfast, and my dad will be very pleased to meet you and get to know you."

"We intended to stay for only a moment, Cole."

"Please, Professor Gordon, it is our pleasure to have you visit and also have breakfast with us. Rani loves a crowd, and she is accustomed to preparing a feast for breakfast, so all of us could not be more pleased."

Al had a broad smile when he entered the living room, "So we have guests for breakfast?"

"Dad, this is Professor Gordon and his son, Graham."

"It is a pleasure to meet you both, and I want to hear all about your adventure in America! Come, let's gather around the dining room table for food and fellowship."

Nya joined them as they took their seats at the table.

"Nya, this is my professor, Mr. Gordon, and his son, Graham." Both gentlemen stood and greeted Nya.

The table was full of an assortment of freshly baked breads, fresh fruit, homemade jams, crispy bacon, homemade yogurt, and freshly squeezed orange juice.

Graham asked for seconds on the hot chocolate. "I cannot help myself, Ms. Rani. This is the best hot chocolate I ever tasted."

Cole said, "Well, you know why? She adds real cream and malt to the milk along with the cocoa. And of course, she tops it off with marshmallows!"

Graham said, "I'm in heaven!"

"We all feel the same way—and all the time," Nya said.

"Folks, we would like to bless the food, and it is our custom to join hands." Al gave thanks, and after a round of "amen," Rani started passing plates of food.

Mr. Gordon shared the highlights of their trip to America and the exceptional medical care that had been given to Graham. The two had stayed for six weeks, and when Graham was released, his eyesight was perfect without any correction. His surgery was successful, and his recovery was complete.

"We felt we had to come see you in person before going back to Oxford. Words cannot adequately express how thankful we are that God brought you, along with this miracle, into our lives."

"Professor Gordon, after breakfast, I would really like to show Graham our horses. I realize horseback riding is probably prohibited for a few more weeks, but I could show him around, and perhaps you both could come visit again later this summer."

"Sure, Cole. I would like to have an opportunity to visit awhile longer with your dad, too."

Nya stood up and said, "Rani, no arguments now. I'm helping you with the kitchen, and there will be no discussion to the contrary!"

Al and Professor Gordon retired to the living room, Cole and Graham headed to the stables, and Rani and Nya thoroughly enjoyed each other's company.

———————

As Graham and Cole walked toward the stables, Graham thought he had never seen a place more serene, beautiful, and stately. Even the grand property of his friend Zina did not hold the magic of this place. Yes, magical was the perfect word for Cole's world. What an interesting and mysterious young man! He seemed ancient in spirit but boyish in looks. He was a carbon copy of his dad, and in some ways the two seemed to have the same wise spirit. He suspected Cole may not have had an opportunity to have a child's life. Certainly, he must have been cast into an adult's world early on. This thought saddened his heart, for he could remember every detail of how great his life was as a young chap. When his mother was still alive, his life was one of laughter, love, and exceptional newness each day. She made life exciting every moment with her creative mind and unbelievable imagination. She was a dreamer, and their world consisted of dreams that came true. He was sure during his challenges with his eyes he survived by living out the past in his thoughts. Yes, the past gave him the will to go on. But Cole seemed to be totally in the moment with great expectations of the future. Something seemed to carry him in a forward motion. As they approached the stables, Graham could hear the horses stirring, as though they anticipated the very presence of Cole.

"Cole, these horses are magnificent."

"They do seem to be exceptional to all of us. Mystery seems part of my own spirit. The first semester I was away from her, she lost weight to the point my dad was concerned about her health and perhaps survival, but when we reunited at Christmas, she seemed to come around, and now she is healthy and happy again!"

"Cole, I have a good friend named Zina, and the entire time I was recovering in America from my surgery, I could not stop thinking about introducing you to her. It would be a huge favor if you could go with me to visit Zina upon your return to Oxford."

"Of course, Graham, I would be happy to visit your friend."

"At one time, she was more than a friend, but circumstances and ill health have destroyed our passions and dreams."

"We can always hope, Graham. Where there is hope, our great God can change things, even restore and renew."

"When I return to Oxford, I plan to visit her straightway, and if she is not better, I may call you."

"I'll help in any way I can, and for now, I shall pray for Zina."

"I know prayer is a big part of your life, Cole. My mom was a woman of great faith, too. After meeting you and your dad and experiencing firsthand the faith that you share as well as the love you both extend, hope has once again stirred in my soul! And I believe this is why I want to introduce you to Zina, for she has little hope."

"Nya plans to visit her folks in New Zealand at some point this summer, and I could come your way at that time. Perhaps in a month or so. We'll pray about God's direction for all of us, Graham. He is a big God and can handle everything. After all, He measured the heavens with His fingers and holds the oceans in His hand. All things are possible with Him."

"When I'm with you, Cole, it is so easy to believe with no doubts."

"It is not me; it is the power of the Holy Spirit. God wants to do great things in your life, Graham. After all, He gave you your eyes back, and not only physical eyes, but I believe He is moving in your heart to give you spiritual eyes."

"Thank you so much for your encouragement, Cole. You are a genuine friend, and I'm so thankful to have you in my life."

# *Chapter 10*

## *Summer's Song*

Cole and Nya were inseparable throughout the beginning of the summer before her departure to New Zealand. Most of their days were spent roaming the meadows and enjoying the magic of the woods with Mystery and Samson. God sang over them in fields and forests and protected them from the pulls and sways of the world. On these excursions, they discovered different places in the woods to spread their blankets, eat their lunches that Rani had lovingly prepared, and read scripture together. After long discussions, they would wrap up in the arms of one another and nap under the grand old oaks with the sun casting dancing energy of light on their pure faces and thirsty souls. Yes, God sang over his children, infused them with truth and light, and prepared them for future events when they would be apart.

Before Dana arrived for her visit, Al bought Cole his first car. He felt it was time Cole became more independent, and the Lamborghini Aventador suited Cole and Nya perfectly. The two made short day trips exploring the countryside before Nya left for New Zealand. They always returned with wind-tossed hair, evidence of plenty of sunshine, and excited about sharing their experiences and discoveries of the day. Cole had been drawn back to his love of photography, and the pictures he took on their day trips were breathtaking! The evening meal was the highlight of Al and Rani's day.

Al and Angelo witnessed the completion of the new ranch house. And as Cole had wished, it was built of stone. European castle stones were shipped in, and the hues were of light tan, reddish brown, and coral, which were joined together with a cream-colored mortar. It was as Cole had imagined. The stallion was moved to the ranch, and Robby spent most of his time getting acquainted with him and breaking him with a gentle hand.

Robby was the happiest he could ever remember. Al suggested he name the stallion, and after pondering for several weeks, Robby named the stallion Ebony Mist and called him "Mist." Robby knew after his first full run atop this great steed, one day he would be the winner of a grand race! Just one win would bring in all the profits that Al would need for a profitable business. Many of the mares at the big house were close to delivering, perhaps a fall of six to eight births. Perfect timing for the colts and fillies to run in the meadow and build their muscles before embracing the winter months being confined to stables. Robby grew happier each day, being in business with Al and knowing that his efforts would make a difference and turn profits. Al had made it plain that this was a partnership, and God above was their leader and employer. Robby knew in his heart this was where he belonged.

There had been a nice article in their local paper about Robby and his new business as a breeder and trainer of racehorses. It was of course Al's idea to keep recognition or credit from targeting himself. In all things, he placed others first, and he knew that Robby needed something to call his own. It brought many of the locals to the new ranch house to have a look at Ebony Mist. And through their networking in the community, calls started coming in about purchasing the first offspring of "The Mist!" Other calls were from people who wanted The Mist to start running in significant races, and one of those races would be held in America the next summer. Al told Robby that all of these types of decisions were not his forte, so Robby would have to say when their stallion was ready for such.

The family continued to serve the Lord in their church, and Al once again helped to expand the sanctuary and also added a coffee shop and cafe for young people to come together and study and share. It seemed to Al whatever dreams God placed in his heart, the Holy Spirit was faithful to show him ways in which he could support others and their community for God's glory. He was a hero in Leeds, and everyone loved him.

Nya had asked Cole to take her to the airport to catch her flight to New Zealand. She also suggested that Dana's arrival coincide with her departure so Dana could have the comforts of her bedroom during her visit and also take Cole's mind off her absence. God made all the crooked places smooth for Nya's departure and Dana's arrival. Cole had been comforted by the fact that Dana's presence and the activity level of her visit would help ease the pain of Nya being ten thousand miles away from him.

Six weeks into the summer, a tearful Nya and a sad Cole sped away in the red sports car, and less than two hours later, Cole returned with Dana, and the joy of the Lord was evident in their reunion.

Upon seeing Dana, Al embraced her warmly, and indeed the radiance of the Lord shone in this woman.

To Rani, she had never seen a more beautiful woman than Dana. Her hair was a golden brown, and her eyes were an emerald green. The indwelling of the Holy Spirit had totally transformed her, and Rani's heart could not stop praising the Lord! She noticed that Al's eyes danced with hope and expectation, and at that moment, in her heart of hearts, she knew Dana and Al were meant to be. All things in God's timing, and He had taken both through many detours since their initial encounter with one another.

Dana beamed as Al and Cole escorted her into their home.

Cole carried her luggage upstairs to Nya's room while Al and Rani visited with Dana downstairs. Cole's heart hurt badly, and tears sprang from his eyes when he saw the special things Nya had organized for Dana's comfort and enjoyment. *Oh my heavenly Father, I am praying for wisdom and perspective and ask you to direct my steps, comfort me in my grief, and calm my fears. Give my sweet Nya traveling mercies, a song in her heart, and unconditional love for her dad and India. May this trip reconnect her to India and connect her with her dad. Sweet Jesus, give them a lasting connection. Nya has been so vulnerable and wounded, and there is nothing that bathes the soul like your love and the love of family. Thank you, precious Lord.*

"Dana, your belongings are in your room on the second floor, right next to Rani's room. May I take the liberty of saddling three horses for us to roam the meadows and trails together?"

"I cannot think of anything I would rather do! Is that okay with you, Al?"

"Certainly, I'll get into my riding clothes. And, Rani, would you mind packing some sandwiches and snacks for us?"

"My pleasure. May you all enjoy this lovely breezy day, and I'll have dinner waiting for you around seven this evening."

Riders and horses were carried on the wings of God's breath that afternoon. It was more than breezy; it was windy! Cole always led the way, with Dana following and Al trailing. The spirits of the horses took on the spirits of their riders, and yes, summer's song was witnessed, felt, and heard … a day to be remembered.

Dana could not contain her excitement over Ebony Mist! After seeing this magnificent animal and listening to Robby expound on his experiences thus far with the young stallion, she knew this horse would shine for the world to witness. They talked extensively about the prospects and details of participating in an American race. Dana knew she could promote The Mist in her magazine, and others would follow. And the beauty of this horse was the fact that his owner was already a hero! Robby needed to hear about Dana's history with regard to western riders. His knowledge was limited in this area, and in order to appeal to the American ranchers, he needed to be still and listen to Dana's experiences and those of her family's as well.

Dana was amazed at the ranch house. It was laid out in such a way that it offered privacy and yet community. The center glassed-in area had an incredible view that elevated one's emotions in such a way that business would be pleasurable, not hard-pressed. Angelo, the architect, had known exactly how to design this place to stimulate the emotional side of business. Everything was extremely well appointed—space, angles, lighting, and views. Dana knew this unique operation brought ranching and horse breeding to a new level.

A week into Dana's visit, Cole received a call from Graham asking him to come to Oxford if possible, on behalf of his friend Zina. Cole was somewhat reluctant, but after discussing it with his dad, he decided to travel back to Oxford. With a heavy heart, he said his goodbyes to his dad, Rani, and Dana. He promised to stay in touch and give them updates until his return.

For some reason Al felt Cole might be gone for a while, but he knew God was directing his path, so he was at peace with his departure.

# Chapter 11

Cole had never seen a grander place. The expanse of green meadows reached the far horizons to the River Thames. The grounds were manicured around the main house, stables, and paddocks. The gardens were artistically designed for the enjoyment of guests. There were tennis courts and swimming pools adjoining the main house to the guest quarters. The manor house was a three-story structure with light gray brick exterior. There were also extensive farm buildings and staff accommodations. But what impressed Cole the most was the green, green pastureland that stretched as far as one could see. It was a rider's paradise! Today, there was a light fog that swept the land as sunlight filtered through and gently rested atop the plush green earth.

*Thank you, Father, for allowing me to see your creation through your eyes and enjoy the bounty of your endless blessings. May this day bring you glory, sweet Jesus.*

Cole parked his car in the circular drive close to the front entrance, and a gray-haired gentleman with a kind smile greeted him and Graham. Cole instantly liked him.

"Mr. Ashton, I would like you to meet a good friend of mine from Leeds. This is Cole Statham. And, Cole, this is Mr. Ashton Ward."

Extending his hand, Cole said, "It is a pleasure to meet you, Mr. Aston."

"And you as well, young man. Welcome to our home."

"Mr. Ashton, I called Zina earlier, and I believe she is expecting us, but she mentioned she would be sleeping in until our arrival. Not sure if she is up to our visit today."

"As you know, Graham, she is never up to anything these days but lying around and dreaming of a better day."

"We can come back later or perhaps tomorrow, if that would be better, Mr. Ashton."

"Oh, no, we would not hear of it. Come on in. Let's go to the small parlor close to the kitchen so I can prepare refreshments for you both. And, gentlemen, please just call me Ashton."

When they were settled in the parlor, Ashton brought tea and delightful pastries and then excused himself to notify Zina of their guests' arrival.

"Graham, this place is absolutely enchanting. How long have you been acquainted with Zina?"

"Perhaps two years."

Zina entered the parlor with grace, but little joy. Cole noted her fragile state.

"Well, hello, Graham. Please introduce me to your guest?"

"Zina, this is Cole Statham. Cole, this is my dear friend Zina."

"Cole, it is a privilege to meet you. Graham has told me all about you and your dad's generosity, and also the incredible visit he had with you and your dad this summer! Would you like for me to have a couple of horses saddled for your riding pleasure this morning while I rest for a while longer?"

Cole was quick to gently say, "Zina, we could come back another time when you are feeling better."

"Unfortunately, Cole, I never feel better. Please stay and enjoy the property and its beauty on horseback. Promise, I will be up to conversing in a few hours. Ashton will have a late lunch prepared upon your return from the meadows, and I'll join you then for a nice visit."

"Cole, let's head to the stables. Remember, Zina, I need a very gentle horse since I am not a gifted rider like you and Cole!"

"Yes, that shall be a major consideration, Graham. You know you can trust me."

---

"Graham, these stables are incredible, and all the horses look to be Arabians."

"You know your breeds, Cole. Indeed they are fine animals. Less than a year ago, there were twice as many as you see now, but after Zina's parents died, she sold at least a half dozen. And of course the stallion was sold, too. He was a beauty. Only Zina could ride him."

"Gentlemen, your horses are ready for you to mount."

"Good morning, Zach. This is my friend, Cole, from Leeds."

"Very nice to meet you, Cole."

"A pleasure meeting you, Zach. Are you the trainer?"

"Why yes, I suppose I am, but there is very little training to be done nowadays. I try to make sure all the horses get the proper exercise, and that's basically how I spend my days. I'm glad the two of you can help me out today! You'll enjoy roaming the pastureland, and you'll find both horses are well suited for walking and running. Both are gentle."

"Thanks, Zach. We'll be off now. See you in a couple of hours. Ready, Cole?"

For as far as one could see, there was beautiful, lush, green pastureland. The two horses settled into a nice smooth walk while Graham told Cole about Zina's life.

"Zina's parents were killed in an automobile accident in May of last year. Both were accomplished researchers, and they were returning from one of their speaking engagements in Australia. When they arrived at the airport, there was a severe storm with fierce winds, and instead of waiting until it passed, they decided to drive home. No one is really certain of the details, but the next morning, their car was discovered at the bottom of a deep ravine, and both were dead. Zina is an only child, and she has been traumatized with failing health since that time. Her parents were devoted to their work and Zina. The three of them were extremely private people. I got to know Zina through my dad. She is very bright and helped him with classroom lectures during her internship. She would have received her PhD the end of that May had her parents remained alive, but she shut down completely. She and I had been enjoying one another's company for over a year, and I would have asked her to marry me if my eyes had not failed me. Both of us were in a deep valley that prohibited us from helping each other. We were consumed by our own misery."

"Graham, have you turned your life over to the Lord and asked Him to direct your steps? I realize this is a direct and personal question, but it will enable me to know God's will in helping both you and Zina."

"Two months ago, I would have said no, but since you and your dad came into our lives, I am certain that I now rely totally on Jesus. I have read the Bible through in the last two months and accept it as the divine Word of God. It was through scripture that I was compelled to ask you to visit Zina, for I know without a doubt an evil spirit has taken over her body."

"My gifts come directly from the Lord either through dreams or visions. I have no formulas, procedures, or methods by which healing comes about for another. At this time, the only thing I can do is share the love of Jesus with Zina and pray for her."

"I understand, Cole, and I hope you know I am not pressuring you to do anything. I just want you to get to know Zina and be her friend."

"Sounds like a plan!"

"Believe it or not, this is one of the few times I've ridden a horse, and I am finding it such a pleasant experience!"

"Wait until you become one with the horse that is beneath you! Even right now I desire to strip the saddle from this horse and ride bareback at top speed across this lush green earth, with my spirit becoming one with this horse's spirit. That is the ultimate thrill for a horse lover, Graham."

"I believe we can accommodate you. Take the saddle from your horse and give it to me. I'll head on back to the stables, and you have yourself a free- spirited run through the meadows and return to the manor at your leisure."

———————

When Cole returned to the manor, Ashton told him Graham was reading in the library on the third floor, and Zina was resting in the sunroom by the pool.

"Zina asked me to direct you to the sunroom. Please take the back hall and join her while I prepare some refreshments for the two of you."

"Come in and have a seat, Cole. How was your ride?"

"It could not have been lovelier. Thanks so much for the wonderful escape. I rode the light gray gelding, and he was totally responsive to body commands. He is a well-trained horse, and I shall always remember my ride this morning. He knows the lay of the land and desires to protect his rider. Truly, I am amazed. It was as though he has known me, even though I am a stranger."

"His name is Gray Mist."

"I find that interesting, as we have a stallion named Ebony Mist!"

"Maybe an omen?"

"Maybe by God's design."

"Graham told me you were a religious sort of a fellow. I would be interested to hear about your beliefs."

"Oh, Ashton, thank you so much for the refreshments. I know Cole is in need of food after his long romp in the meadows!"

"Yes, thank you, Ashton."

"Will that be all, Miss Zina?"

"I believe so. Please do see that Graham is comfortable upstairs."

"I shall."

"Zina, I do want to share many aspects of my life with you, but more than anything, I want to hear your story and get acquainted with where your heart is right now."

"Where *is* my heart? That's a good question, Cole. Do you know, have you seen, could you help me search? I laid it down, I threw it away, it was no good and could not stay. It clouded my judgment, taxed my mind, bound my desires, and blinded my eyes. It was prideful but hopeful that freedom and love would prevail. The dreams and passion flourished for a season and then crumbled and failed. The seasons have come and gone, and now what remains are eyes that are dim and memories recalled through rivers of tears. Do you think your God can free me of the conflict within my soul and heal my heart?"

"Zina, I believe you could be mired in the past. I've lived through conflicts and trials similar to yours and found that God's grace forgives and frees, and His pursuit of us is relentless."

"Whatever is pursuing me is taking me under, and I feel that I am in a downward spiral that consumes every thought, every movement, and has me totally imprisoned in my pain."

"So your pain is physical and mental?"

"I am held captive in this body that has become useless to me. There is little I can enjoy because of the effort it takes. Can your God help me?"

"Perhaps my story may help you to understand God's grace and desire for all of His children, you included."

As he shared experiences in his life from the time he was a little boy to present day, Zina became receptive and shared her life's experiences as well.

They talked nonstop until Graham appeared in the doorway.

"Hope I am not interrupting, but we should probably go and give Zina a chance to rest. Cole, you must take a look at the sun setting in the west. There are few sunsets that continue forever like the ones here."

"Oh, yes, I would love to see! Zina, we have covered quite a bit of territory today. Why don't you give me a call when you are up to another visit?"

"Cole, I cannot thank you enough. I'll be in touch with you both."

As the two young men walked outside, their figures could be seen against the backdrop of a sky that was created straight from heaven by the finger of God. The heavens seemed to have swallowed the earth with God's power, majesty, and sovereignty. Truly, a sight that simply could not be described. One could only witness.

———⁓⁓⊶⊶⊙⊶⊶⁓⁓———

Cole sat on the balcony of his apartment. It was a simple abode with a living area downstairs and a bedroom with adjoining bath upstairs. The balcony was nestled close to the top of a live oak tree, and on this night, the moon was hanging like an orange orb in the distance. The longer he looked at the moon, the more it seemed to throb with a heartbeat of its very own.

*Oh, Lord, how I covet to abide in your Spirit of truth at all times. I do desire to help Zina, and at the same time, I recognize that she has to cooperate with your Spirit through times of pain and suffering so you can guide her. We all are to be refined and transformed to prepare us to truly be your vessel, but, Lord, it is no easy task for us humans. Please give me discernment, dear Lord.*

Right before dawn, Cole was awakened. Someone was calling his name over and over from a great distance. He wondered if Nya was in some kind of distress. His phone was on, but no calls registered. "What could it be?" He dozed back off to sleep, and again he heard his name. *Lord, if this is of you, I'm listening.* He felt a cold chill in the room. *In the Name of Jesus, get thee behind me, Satan.* He turned on the bedside lamp and grabbed his Bible.

———⁓⁓⊶⊶⊙⊶⊶⁓⁓———

Zina reflected on her visit with Cole while she sipped on a cup of tea Ashton had brought to her bedside. Cole was certainly a strange one but most likable. He was very comfortable with himself, more so than anyone she had ever met. In some ways, he seemed so pure and innocent, and other ways so old and wise. He was an enigma to her for sure! She really wanted to share the truth about herself with him but surmised he may not understand since they did not have a history together. Graham mentioned to her that perhaps Cole was gifted with supernatural powers. She had to admit she was intrigued to the point of asking Graham to bring Cole for a visit, and now she wanted more than anything for him to visit again! Just this morning, she again experienced trying to come out of her sleep and having to struggle with all her might to come out of a deep darkness that pulled her downward. It was as though it would be easier to die than live. It had been like this since her parents were killed in the accident. She was always fearful of going to sleep because of what she would have to endure in the mornings. Lately, whenever she napped during the day, she had the same struggle trying to wake up. She knew she was full of fear but did not want to admit it to herself and certainly not to anyone else. *How does one fight with fear? How can fear be overcome? What causes fear? What do I fear?* This was a record she played over and over in her mind. This morning, the pain all over her body was so great she seemed immobilized. The cup of tea felt as though it weighed five pounds. Her head pounded, and every nerve in her body throbbed. She called out to Ashton.

"Yes, Zina, are you ready for breakfast?"

"No, I am not. Sorry, Ashton. I know you try so hard to do everything you can to make my life better, but nothing helps. Would you do me a favor and call Cole, the young man who visited yesterday? He left his phone number on the coffee table in the sunroom."

"Of course I'll call him. When would you prefer he visit?"

"Now."

"I'll give him a call right away."

As Cole drove up to the manor, he could not help wondering what the urgency was regarding a visit so soon again. Ashton had seemed quite anxious when he requested Cole drive over immediately.

When Cole stepped out of his car, Ashton greeted him with a smile and yet a perplexed brow.

"Cole, thank you for coming over on such short notice. I am very concerned about Zina. To be honest with you, she seems to escape reality more with each passing day. This morning, she is deeply distressed, but knowing her, she will try to pretend that she is doing okay. Anyway, she took the elevator to the third floor and is sitting in the library by the window. This is a delightful day, is it not?"

"Ashton, it is a glorious day that our Lord has created for us to enjoy!"

As Cole approached the doorway of the library, Zina stood and greeted him with a gracious smile.

"Thank you for coming to visit, Cole."

"Ashton is quite concerned about you. Are you okay this morning?"

"I'm making an effort to be. Please come have a seat here in the sunlight. Don't you love the morning sun?"

"I do. The eastern sky is my favorite."

"It is an odd thing, Cole, but when you are close to me, I have hope that I shall be all right."

"I believe you are going to be okay, Zina."

"You know what I would like for us to do today?"

"Your wish is my command."

"Let's have Zach prepare Gray Mist and Autumn Spirit for us to take a morning ride."

"Are you sure you are up to riding, Zina?"

"Never sure, always fearful, but this is what we shall do this morning. It will only take me a few minutes to change into riding clothes. Please tell Ashton to prepare us lunches to take with us. I want to ride out to the edge of our property by the river."

"Okay, if you are sure."

Ashton had been on an emotional roller coaster since the death of Mr. and Mrs. Godwin. He had served his masters for over twenty years, and they had been loyal to him and loved him. Now, each day was one of total uncertainty with Zina. He knew he would always stay and try to take care of her as long as she would allow. He had no family, and the Godwins had treated him like family for all the years of his employment.

Yes, he was dedicated to taking care of Zina regardless of the heartaches and difficulties.

"Greetings again, Ashton. Zina would like for you to prepare lunches for us to take on a ride today."

"This is highly unusual, Cole. Are you sure you can take care of her?"

"I'll do my best. Apparently she has not ridden in a while, right?"

"Not since the death of her parents."

"Sir, I am praying about all of this, and I know God's hand is directing us. I'm headed to the stables to help Zach saddle two of the horses."

Zina was amazed that she had suggested riding horses. What was happening to her? There was no change in her body, for it was weak and unwilling, but her spirit was elevated and even motivated. She felt almost giddy with Cole and was experiencing a sense of freedom as she had not felt since losing her parents. *My life could change. It is possible. Perhaps Cole is my miracle, as Graham had hoped.* There was just something about him that gave her a fearless desire to abandon who she had become over the past year. Actually, she no longer knew the trapped person she had become. She had to escape or die!

Cole led the horses to the front entrance so Zina would not have far to walk. Ashton met him with a backpack full of goodies and a most apprehensive and concerned look.

Zina walked gingerly toward Autumn, and Cole helped her to mount.

"Ashton, you are much too serious. You must lighten up for my sake. If I can manage this ride, it will be a major feat and huge step forward toward my healing. Please do not worry. I love you for caring so much, but I need your encouragement and confidence to help me break free from being imprisoned by mental and physical restraints this past year."

"Of course, you are right. I'll do my best. Now, go and enjoy this glorious day!"

They rode at an easy pace for at least a half mile before coming to a halt and resting.

"How do you like Autumn, Cole?"

"She looks like a new copper penny in the sunlight, and her gait is the smoothest I've ever seen. I'm guessing she is a walker?"

"Actually, an American Saddlebred horse. We bought her a couple of years ago from a ranch in America. I have loved her gentleness and yet powerful presence. Plus she has five smooth gaits that offer the most heavenly ride ever!"

"She is a beauty. You'll have to give me the details later of where you purchased her. I know my dad would love to incorporate this breed into his business."

"We only have another half mile or so before we reach the river. Have you ever seen a more glorious day or bluer sky, Cole?"

"No, and it does my heart good to see you enjoying the moment."

"Cole, you hardly know me, and yet you thoroughly know me. How can that be?"

"Zina, it is best to just be in the moment at God's command with what He gives us to enjoy. I have no desire to analyze or speculate about tomorrow or next week. We have this day that God has given us, and to really live and be a blessing is to give our spirits the gift of just being. Does that make sense?"

"Yes, it does, Cole. Thank you for helping me to live in the moment. More than anything, I would like to turn loose of the past. I believe you have come into my life to help me embark on a new journey."

"Well, I am here to help you, and I only live fifteen minutes away."

# *Chapter 12*

Dana's visit was coming to an end. She had two more days with Al and Rani before she returned to the States. When she thought about leaving, her heart jumped to her throat, and warm tears filled her eyes. Now she understood how Vera felt when she did not want to leave Conner. An ocean apart is another world to one's heart. She had been with Al only nineteen days, but it seemed like a lifetime.

She and Al had planned to meet with Robby before she departed to further discuss how to bring serious ranchers from America to Leeds to purchase the offspring of Ebony Mist. She felt confident the business plan was on target to produce profits within a year of initial start-up with the stallion. He was without a doubt the most incredible horse she had ever seen. She also knew the right technique of marketing Al's business would bring about a huge success. Al had no need to make money for himself but desired to invest and promote for the success of others. She saw this firsthand with Robby. He was simply not the same man she had met a little over a year ago. Yes, he was humble, kind, and sincere, but more than anything, he was filled with expectancy and hope. Perhaps hope to realize that the dreams God places deep in our hearts will come true.

She poured her second cup of coffee and pondered many things in her heart. Rani had slept in this morning, and apparently Al had as well. This morning the gardens were especially enjoyable with a light dust of dew that danced with rainbow colors in the tiny spider webs woven between the rose bushes. The roses were as beautiful as the tender care they received from Rani's green thumb.

"Good morning, early bird."

"Good morning to you. Come have a seat beside me and enjoy that first cup of coffee!"

"I will. Starting our day in the gardens with morning coffee is as good as it gets, right?"

"I can think of a few things that might top it!"

"I'm listening."

"I guess at this point I would have to say extending my vacation time to stay in England longer!"

"Here, let's take a departure from our coffee time and walk through the gardens."

"Oh, Al, my heart hurts when I think about my life in the States. Being here with you and Rani has been the dream of a lifetime. I have witnessed generosity, love, unselfishness, and just the true spirit of Christ in this family and community. I shall never forget how the Lord changed my life through you, Al Statham!"

"You'll have to admit the first part of our journey was rocky with extreme detours, but I believe God refined his raw materials into a beautiful and lasting connection."

"Dana, I have come to realize over the past two weeks how much I desire you to always be a part of our lives here in Leeds. And I believe you feel a strong bond with us as well."

"I do, Al."

"Even though our ages have quite a gap, I know God brought us together for His purpose, and I would like for you to consider my proposal and pray about it. I feel in my spirit you and I should take a month or so to pray and ponder, for this could change both of our lives forever, especially yours."

"Yes, Al, prayer is essential, especially about decisions that will affect the rest of our lives."

"I want us to consider being partners for life and one with God. Do you desire the same, Dana?"

"Oh, Al, I do, more than anything."

His dark auburn hair glistened in the morning sun, and hers shone like spun gold. The two embraced and kissed amid the dew-covered roses. God had brought them together in His divine design and timing.

Rani had come downstairs and witnessed their embrace from the window. *Dear Father in heaven, these two deserve one another. I know you will do great things through their union. Both have hearts set apart for your service, and I know both of them desire to be in your perfect will. Guide them through your precious Holy Spirit. May each be a healing balm to the other's heart, for I know they have had tremendous heartache. Father, we know that "shared joy is a double joy; shared sorrow is half a sorrow," so bless their union and join them as one with you. Thank you, our awesome, merciful, and loving Father.*

———⟶ᴡᴏᴏ◦◦ᴏᴏ⟵———

The dinner Rani prepared for Dana's last night was the best. Actually, all of her meals could be considered her best. She did everything as if she were preparing whatever she touched for the king's table. She served the Lord with her heart, mind, time, and hands. Conner, Vera, and Austin had joined them for farewells.

Al had shared with everyone that he and Dana were praying about getting married and would appreciate their prayers regarding God's will for them.

Nobody was surprised over this news, least of all Vera. She had known since she and Dana met that Dana's heart belonged to Al. Once Dana released her false pride, everything God had planned for her life fell into place.

After everyone said their goodbyes, Al and Dana changed into riding clothes and went to the stables. There was a full moon overhead and a breeze encircling them with the fragrances of Rani's roses. The night was magical, and both were overjoyed by their love for one another. Al rode Rapha, the buckskin, and Dana rode Mystery. Both horses sprang out of the stables, and as soon as their riders had securely mounted, the two were in a full run across the meadow toward the woods. The two dismounted when they reached the woods, tethered the horses, and strolled by the moss-covered creek. Overhead the breeze had its way with the tops of the large oaks, and night sounds became magnified and created enchantment in the forest. Al pulled Dana close to him.

"I love you, Dana, with all my heart."

"I love you, too, Al, and have for a very long time."

Nature's symphony pulsed with one heartbeat, and Al and Dana both knew God had joined them together forever.

———⟶ᴡᴏᴏ◦◦ᴏᴏ⟵———

Dana had been back in the States for over a month. True to what she and Al had agreed upon, she had prayed diligently to God about His direction for her life. Each day opened up new doors, and one by one she lived that day with little thought of the next. She had shared with her boss, Mr. Davidson, that there was a good possibility she would be moving to England. Both had chuckled when he said there would have to be future restrictions regarding his female employees traveling to England!

She had also written an article about Al's new business and the bloodline of Ebony Mist. Just the photographs alone would promote curiosity and interest.

Robby had called her to say there were several inquiries already. He mentioned that two American ranchers named Clay Samuels and Alan Marshall were making plans to visit.

She had also spoken to her parents on several occasions about her plans to marry Al and move to England. They had remembered Cole as a little boy and seemed genuinely happy for her. She and Al had discussed having a very small wedding with just family. She knew his first wedding had been a special event, and she did not desire for hers to diminish anything from Al's first ceremony. Al was such a tenderhearted individual, and he was generous to a fault. He would give her the world; she knew it, and that was enough. Both had agreed that Thanksgiving would be a special time to get married. Cole could come home for the holidays, and her folks could get a couple of the neighboring families to handle the chores at their ranch for a week. Al had mentioned that Rani would be in her element, handling details of the wedding and reception to follow. The more the two of them talked on the phone, the more deeply they cared for one another. They greeted each other in the morning, spoke of details and events during the day, and said good night before retiring each night. At times, Al seemed like an excited teenage boy going on his first date. His innocence thrilled her heart and made her love him all the more. To know Al Statham was to love him. He was respected and admired by so many people, but most of all he was loved.

# Chapter 13

Cole and Graham had spent the evening together having a leisure dinner and rather lengthy visit. Cole had shared a detailed progress report about Zina. He shared the fact that on the mornings Zina invited him to visit, he always heard his name being called in his sleep before awakening. He knew it was God's divine intervention but could not unravel it. He and Zina had talked hours on end about every aspect of their individual lives. They had read the Bible together, and he knew she trusted Jesus as her Savior. Her faith had been placed in action over the last several weeks. No matter how weak she felt, her spirit was very strong, and she was filled with the joy of the Lord. She had spoken on several occasions about how she dreaded to go to sleep at night for fear of not waking up in the morning. She said trying to wake up was the hardest thing she did, for there was always a force that wanted to pull her down, and it would be easier to let go and not face another day. The more he thought of this, the more he believed that as she called out in desperation, he heard his name being called in his sleep. Zina could be holding on to God through him. "Yes, that must be it!"

*Dear Father, help Zina to realize she needs you and you alone. Lord, you are her source of comfort, not me. You are her source, not me. Help her to realize that what she is attracted to in me is really you. Oh, Lord, how I miss my Nya. Truly, we are worlds apart, but my heart still beats as one with hers. Thank you for reconnecting her with family. Please bring her back to me in your timing, dear Lord.*

---

Again, he heard his name called from a distance. He arose, got dressed, and went to Zina. Aston met him at the front entrance with great urgency.

"Cole, please hurry. Zina had nightmares all through the night, and this morning she seems to be in such a deep sleep I cannot rouse her!"

Cole hurried to Zina's bedroom, knowing in his heart that God would break the evil one's grip.

"Zina, you are a child of God. Be healed in the Name of Jesus." He grabbed her and picked her up from her bed.

"Ashton, open the shades and the windows. Bring as much light in here as you possibly can.

"Be healed, Zina; be healed in the Name of Jesus."

At first it was only a breeze. Then a strong wind and light swirled all around them. The wind stopped at once, and the light was embraced with dead silence.

Zina looked amazingly radiant and somewhat surprised to find herself in the arms of her hero.

"Cole, you saved me once again."

"Zina, our Lord God saved you and healed you of your weakness and fear. He has released you from the attack of the evil one. You are free. Stand and feel God's strength surging through your body. Claim this victory for Christ."

"Oh, Cole, Ashton, how amazing I feel. I'm me again. I've been gone for so long and fought so hard, so very hard. Oh, my Lord, I glorify you this glad day! We must celebrate our Lord this day. Ashton, you look so pale. Are you okay?"

"I'm more than okay. I just witnessed a miracle!"

---

Cole spent the remainder of the day with Zina. She truly was a different person than the young woman he had witnessed over the past few weeks. God will forever be in the business of bringing about miracles when we believe, really believe.

When he returned to his apartment that evening, he called Graham and asked him to come by for a progress report. Graham was not surprised about Zina's healing. His faith was etched in the truth, just as Cole's was. They dined together and talked past midnight. Cole spoke of his love for Nya and how much he missed her. Graham understood, for he had missed

Zina for a year or more. As the two sat on the balcony, the moon shone on their faces. Faces full of eternal glorious hope.

"Now, Graham, my journey with Zina ends, and yours resumes. Zina's healing will be a healing for you, too, my friend. Perhaps you can go to her in the morning and celebrate with her! This is a promising passage for you both. May the Holy Spirit lead you into a life of overflow with His confidence. And may our gracious heavenly Father join you and Zina in His love and peace. I have decided to remain here until the fall semester begins. I need some time and space to myself, perhaps a personal retreat. I would very much like to be untethered from earthly missions for a short season and just rest in the mighty Spirit of God, a time of intense worship and praise. Does that sound selfish?"

"Oh, Cole, not at all. You and your dad are just alike. You always have your antennas out to help all those in need, and I totally understand your wanting to draw in and have alone time with God. You need to refuel your tank, Cole!"

"Yes, I believe you summed it up well. I need to refuel, and nothing but the very breath of God can accomplish such for me!"

"So, you've definitely decided not to go back home before school starts?"

"That's correct. My dad is busy right now with his new ranching venture, and he is making plans to be married during the Thanksgiving holidays, so I'll be going home then."

"Congratulations to your dad. Hope you are in favor of this union."

"I am totally okay with it. He is marrying Dana Fulton from St. Louis, Missouri, and she is one of the nicest individuals you could ever meet. I met her when I was a young boy, and she took me to visit her family's ranch in Montana. I shall never forget her tenderness, patience, and kindness. She has been in love with my dad for a very long time. God transformed her life, and she will make the perfect wife for my dad!"

# Chapter 14

Nya flipped back through a dozen or so pages of her journal. This had been the longest entry yet:

My dearest Cole, we are still one, my love, even though we are oceans apart and in many ways worlds apart. I have had a full and rich time here with India and Dad. Both of them have shown me love and tenderness. I've seen a side of them that I never witnessed when we were in England. At first I was cool and indifferent, but after a few days of seeing genuine love expressed between them and sincere efforts to embrace me, I found that all my resentment melted away. We have had heart-to-heart talks about the past, and late-night talks about the joys in our experiences each day we're together. I feel as though this journey completes my healing, a healing I've coveted since I was a small child. So many of the puzzle pieces have finally come together.

I've wondered about you, your dad, and Rani every day I've been here. You know I left a piece of my soul with all of you in Leeds. I've wondered about the girl who Graham asked you to help. At times my heart races with doubts, and I have to pray for the peace of Jesus, especially when I think you could be taken from me. I want more than ever to rest in His confidence regarding our eternal bond. I have such freedom in my spirit living here with Dad and India. I am taking online courses and shall continue until

I return to Leeds this next summer. Will we be able to be away from one another for a whole year? I never dreamt this could be the case, but there is a part of me that needs quality time with my family, and in my heart of hearts, I'm confident you'll wait on me. And should you not, then so be it; I shall live my life out alone, for you, my darling Cole, are the only one for me during this earthly journey.

Rani called me last week and said your dad and Dana were getting married at the house the Sunday after Thanksgiving. How I rejoice in this union. I believe this is a match made in heaven. Please forgive me for not coming home for the wedding or Christmas. You may not understand, but I know you'll abide sweetly by my wishes with no pressure. Dad bought some gentle retired thoroughbreds, and we enjoy riding them in the most beautiful settings. We have a trailer, and the horses are most cooperative about loading up, and then off we go to the most scenic places on earth to ride! There have been endless days of beauty, laughter and bonding. When I see you I shall tell you more of our experiences.

I hope you call soon. Seems you've been occupied, and once school starts, you'll be ever more occupied with your debate team. I pray this year will be rewarding for you, both personally and academically. Our lives are changing, aren't they, my love? I miss Mystery and Samson. I know they are receiving excellent care, but how I miss being atop Mystery in a full run across the meadow.

I've wondered about Robby. He will always be family to me. My mother depended on him. In many ways, he was her companion rather than my dad. I've come to the realization that she was just a little child in an adult body. She was her happiest with Robby and me. Dad was not capable of offering her emotional support, and she was unable to emotionally support my dad. Their union, as strange as it was, created a little girl who grew to be a woman, and that woman loves a man named Cole Statham with all her heart and soul.

Oh, my love, some nights my pillow is wet with tears before I finish praying for you and thanking our Lord for bringing you into my life. Take time for yourself, Cole. Enjoy the blue sky, the lush green trees, the sunrises, sunsets, the sounds of the wind, and the fragrance of the rain. Listen to the gentle whispers of Jesus guiding you into His fresh revelations daily and never cease to love Him with all your heart. I ache to my very bone marrow, for I miss you more than life. To be in your space, touch your flesh, and breathe your air is my deepest desire. Oh that God would tame this fire in me or I shall be consumed.

*Dear Father, protect Cole and comfort him. May your glory continue to be revealed in all he does. Sweet Jesus, keep us pure for one another until the appointed day you unite us. I ask these things in the Name of Jesus. Amen.*

———⌇⌇⌇⌇⌇———

After registering and glancing over debate topics for the first semester, Cole decided to drive to Bantham Beach in Devon. He slipped his journal in his overnight bag, locked the door behind him, and sensed a freedom that he had never known. He had driven close to four hours before he stopped in a little fishing village. The wonderful smells of fresh grilled fish led him to a little cafe where food was served outside, and he could watch the fishing boats proudly present their catch at day's end. He observed old men with strong bodies straining with their nets. Many of the sights of the little fishing villages took him back in time, for technology had not awakened them to a different life, and this made Cole long in the deepest part of his soul for simplicity and purity. He ordered a grilled fish sandwich, dill pickles, and a large lemonade. The fresh air had given him an enormous appetite, so he decided to have a slice of apple pie with melted cheese on top as well. He enjoyed the setting sun, the smells, the sounds, and just being in the moment. The waitress had told him there was only one inn in the little village, but it was clean and owned by a family that had always lived there. He thanked her, drove to the inn, and settled in for the night. He fell asleep as soon as he turned his end table lamp off.

———————

Gleaming sun rays shining through the small opening in his window shade announced the new day that dawned before him. He stretched and reached for his Bible, pen, and journal. He felt somewhat remiss when he took note of his last journey entry.

He had talked to Nya the day he returned from seeing Zina after her supernatural healing. They spoke only briefly, as she and her dad were loading up the horses for a ride.

> My precious Nya, today I will explore the golden beach and dunes of Bantham in Devon. I stayed in an old inn last night and slept wonderfully well ... no dreams or visions, just sweet rest. There is a fierce wind stirring outside this morning, so the ocean tide will be roaring and speaking of ancient times to my soul.
>
> When I think about all those I hold so dear—you, Dad, Rani—it seems I am worlds away from all of you. Right now I covet to be held closely and quietly in the strong hand of our Lord. I wish to have no thoughts of the future whirling around in my head, just the sweet peace of Jesus. This may sound strange for me to say, but I need a sabbatical from people. Yesterday, when I was observing the fishermen at the dock, I longed to be one with the sea as they appeared to be. I'm sure they have daily activities that are exactly the same each day, and yet their spirits are fed afresh from God's mighty works. Their smiles were genuine, their conversation joyful, and their bodies were

strong. I have never been one who could go to sleep at night knowing the following day would be the same as the day before. Even though I rest in the Lord, there is always an underlying expectancy about tomorrow. I could sum up my life thus far by saying it is not *my* life.

I have thoughts at times about my commitment to you. You know my life is not an easy one, and yet you've never questioned your future with me. Nya, do you want to commit to an earthly journey with me? We may never be able to make plans in our lives as most couples do. There will always be uncertainty, surprises, and detours as we surrender ourselves to God's bidding. I am certain I will never love another as I love you, Nya. In my heart, you are always one with me. The dreams God places in my heart are our dreams, not just mine. Whenever the Holy Spirit reveals things, I feel strongly that you are part of the equation. Since I met you, I have lived as two joined. I believe we were born to breathe as one and serve the Lord together, always. When we come together again, we should discuss all aspects of a future commitment and ask the Lord to give us clarity and a heavenly perspective. I will look for your beautiful face in the clouds today. I will rejoice in the whispers of the wind and delight myself in the warmth of the sun. Nya, I carry you constantly in my heart. Be safe, my beloved, and feel my arms holding you close. How I love you.

# *Chapter 15*

Robby was busier than ever before, and he and Al felt confident their efforts would bring about an interesting and profitable ranching business. Dana had worked hard in the States to promote their Ebony Mist. Actually, if it were not for her marketing abilities, he would not be preparing for the arrival of Clay Samuels and Alan Marshall.

The Mist had already made his claim to fame on several racecourses in the area. A young jockey had been employed by the name of Grafton Mitchell. Mitch had a horse whisperer quality about him, and Robby felt he would instinctively know how far he could push and when to let up regarding The Mist's practice races. Robby had suggested to Al that Mitch stay in the trainer's quarters at the ranch house. It seemed elaborate for such a youngster, but Robby just felt more comfortable in his home, and since it was not far from the ranch house, he knew it would work well. Mitch was on the quiet side and a gentle soul. Any interactions he had with guests would be minimal. His main concern would be communicating with Robby about the changes, development, and progress of The Mist.

Surprisingly, all but two colts had been sold for handsome prices. As soon as they were weaned, their owners would be transporting them. One of the colts looked identical to Ebony, except for a white mark on his forehead. The mark looked very much like a cross. Robby had never seen such. He knew this colt would be remarkable.

Conner had gone to the airport to bring Clay and Alan to the ranch house. Rani had arrived to attend to the details for the meals, and roses had been cut and placed in all rooms of the house. All had been set in motion, and Robby could hardly believe these two men were traveling this far to express interest in The Mist and his offspring. He could remember so many times he dared to dream of such a life as a horse trainer, and now God had granted him favor.

*Lord, I give you all the honor and glory. May all guests who visit our ranch see your hand in all things, and may lives be changed for your purposes, dear Jesus.*

Rani greeted the guests at the beautiful glass entry as soon as they arrived. She was such a bright star with silver hair, face aglow, and a radiant smile. Who could resist her?

Conner gave Rani a hug and introduced Clay and Alan.

"Welcome, young Americans. We are thrilled you have come to visit us!"

Both young men extended their hands to Rani.

"And here is your host, Robby."

"Clay, Alan, so good to see you both. I trust your flight was uneventful and quite safe?"

"Indeed. Everything has been extraordinarily smooth thus far," said Clay.

"Please come on in, and I'll escort you to your quarters. Conner and I will bring your luggage while you catch your breath. I have placed the two of you in bedrooms in the left wing of the house closest to the stables."

"Rani, what are your plans for refreshments?"

"Gentlemen, get yourselves settled in, and I'll have plenty for your hardy appetites when you return to the living area here."

Alan could not contain his excitement. "Truly, I have never seen such a well-appointed ranch house. The design of this place is magnificent. I have to say I am overwhelmed!"

Clay smiled. "I believe this is going to be our best vacation yet!"

Conner said, "You may want to extend your stay a few more days. Two days here will not scratch the surface of what there is to delight your soul and bring joy to your spirit!"

Clay and Alan smiled at one another and shook their heads in amazement.

—⁓⦾⦿⦾⁓—

It had been a bombastic day for the guys. Mitch joined Robby when he took Clay and Alan to the stables where the mares and Ebony's offspring were. They were mesmerized by Victory. Robby had given the colt with the cross on his forehead the temporary name of Victory, and the other colt that had not been sold, he named Spirit.

Victory and Spirit had put on quite a show, running and bucking in the meadow. Victory was drawn to Clay. When Clay tried to give his attention to the other horses, Victory would place his little head under Clay's arm. The general consensus was a match made in heaven!

Robby had known they would sell only one of the colts, and Victory was Al's choice to keep. Al thought the cross on Victory's head was a reminder of God's grace and mercy.

Back at the ranch house, Rani had prepared her usual, a meal fit for a king. Both Clay and Alan's eyes lit up. Robby had asked Conner and Mitch to join them as well. Rani placed all the platters and pitchers around the dining room table and excused herself.

"This is a man's night out, so you guys have yourself a great evening. Place the dishes in the kitchen sink, and I'll be back to take care of things in the morning. Breakfast will be served at seven, and coffee will be ready at six thirty. Enjoy your evening."

Everyone thanked Rani as she departed.

After the meal was finished and dishes placed in the sink, everyone retired to the great room. The moon hung low and could be seen through the large panels of glass.

"Robby, you are a fortunate horse trainer. This place would be every rancher's dream," Clay announced.

"Yes, Clay, I am very blessed. The Lord has shown me much favor, and I am humbled."

Alan asked, "What about your boss, Mr. Statham?"

"That is a question that encompasses some large territory. Trying to sum up Al Statham is an impossible task."

Alan said, "Give it your best shot."

Conner said, "I'll share a few things I know about Al. He is generous, kind, fair, totally unselfish, a rock in our community, well respected, and loved. He loves the Lord with all his heart, and he always places others above himself."

Alan was speechless.

Mitch chimed in, "I know I am the new kid on the block and young at that, but Mr. Statham treats me with great respect and listens to my opinions with sincere interest as though I've had years of experience. He treats me like his equal. I really admire him."

"I agree," Robby said. "And I'll tell you something else. He has raised his son, Cole, to be the same way. Both of them have a heart set apart for the Lord."

"It is wonderful doing business with fellow Christians," Clay said.

Alan agreed.

Robby asked, "Well, since you guys have been in the horse business at least as long as I have, what do you think Ebony Mist's chances are if we enter him in the Kentucky Derby next May?"

Alan said, "I believe if you and Mitch continue to train him with confidence and win his total trust, Mitch can lead him to a victory at the Derby!"

Clay added, "I'm sure you'll have plenty of press, and your fans will be pulling for all of you. The Mist is a spirited horse, and he'll not want mud flying in his face. I would predict that he will lead the race from beginning to finish."

Robby smiled and said, "Your opinions are respected, and I hope that Mitch and I can make every day and every opportunity count. Now, what do you think about the colts? I know you came here hoping to purchase a prize to take back to America!"

"Yes," Alan said. "We hope to have a stallion at our ranch that is equal to Ebony Mist. Clay and I have worked long and hard the last few years to build a successful ranching business that would provide for our families. Our dad helped us with the initial investment, and just this last year, we've repaid him and hope we have enough to purchase Ebony's colt, Victory!"

Robby paused and said, "Purchasing Victory may not be possible, for that is the colt that has won the heart of Mr. Statham."

Clay said, "Would it be possible for us to perhaps visit with Mr. Statham tomorrow and discuss the matter?"

Robby said, "Of course. I'm confident he would enjoy visiting with the two of you. I'll give him a call tonight, and I'll let you know in the morning what time we can meet with him. Sound okay?"

Both agreed. "Sounds great!"

Conner and Mitch stood up at the same time.

Conner shook Alan's and Clay's hands. "It has been a pleasure, and I hope to see more of you two over the weekend."

Mitch said his goodbyes and departed to his quarters.

"Well, guys, I'm leaving the house to you. Enjoy your breakfast in the morning. Promise it will be another feast! I have chores to do at the house, so I'll come by after breakfast, and hopefully we'll meet with Mr. Statham. Night to you, both."

"Good night, Robby, and thanks for your gracious hospitality," Clay said as he shook Robby's hand.

"See you in the morning," Alan said.

———~w∞⊙⟨⊙⟩⊙⊙∞w———

Clay was awakened by the crow of a rooster; it felt just like home. He smiled as he thought about the interesting people he had met at the ranch house. All of them had hearts for the Lord. That in itself was unusual in businesses. He could not imagine the start-up investment in an operation like Mr. Statham's. The success of this man was matchless. It would be most interesting to hear his testimony.

Alan tapped on his door. "Get your lazy self out of the bed, and let's waste no time. We only have today to make this deal!"

"Let's not forget that God is in control, Alan."

"Well, we're in the right place for that to happen, are we not? I am amazed at how all of the people we've met thus far obviously place God first in their lives. Kind of reminds you of our family commitments, doesn't it?"

"I find this place, the people, and the experiences of yesterday astounding."

"Let's get our morning coffee and go out to the courtyard and enjoy the sunrise. This place is a paradise!"

———~w∞⊙⟨⊙⟩⊙⊙∞w———

Mitch was up early and getting The Mist ready for a practice race around the track. He loved riding first thing in the morning when the fog was breaking. The Mist was always ready to run, and in the mornings, he was especially spirited, wanting complete freedom to run top speed.

Mitch noticed that the Americans were sitting in the courtyard, and he knew seeing The Mist run at top speed this morning would probably clinch the decision to buy one of the colts.

"Okay, Ebony Mist, you are the wind, you are free. Now run as never before!"

When he let him have his head, the horse leaped into action unexpectedly, and he almost lost his balance. Rough start for him but magnificent start for Ebony.

Before Alan and Clay saw the horse, they heard a thundering pounding of hooves, and then out of the mist they saw Ebony running faster than they had ever witnessed a horse run, and with the ease and grace of an accomplished thoroughbred that could run forever.

"Clay, I cannot believe my eyes!"

"Nor can I."

"Think about it. This horse is only two and a half. What will he be like at three?"

"Alan, I am praying we can come to an agreement with Mr. Statham on the purchase of one of those colts."

"Clay, we do need to let God have control of this. I cannot imagine the asking price of Ebony's offspring, can you?"

"Not after what we just witnessed!"

———～w∾⌒⌒⌒⌒∽∾ww——

True to his word Robby stopped by after breakfast and mentioned he had been in touch with Mr. Statham. They were expected at the big house that morning around ten.

Al had pondered and prayed about what God would have him say to Clay and Alan. He knew when Robby approached him about two Americans coming to visit that the past could easily slip into the present. Of course, Robby did not understand Al's reluctance about the Americans' visit until he shared more of the details about his past. But Robby had convinced him to not let Satan steal an opportunity where God's purposes could bring glory. Robby was a wise and good man, his best friend, too.

He had a fitful night's sleep, so he slept late into the morning. He missed Rani's early morning fellowship and the smell of coffee coming from the kitchen long before he embraced the day. God had gifted her with such nurturing qualities, and he loved her as though she were his mother. The unpleasant dreams of last night gave way to praise, and he knew his apprehension was lifting as the sun's rays lifted the fog.

*Oh, Lord, help me to always give the reins of control to you. My past will forever trip me up if I look at myself in the flesh. Only can I be at peace when I live in the moment where you can be glorified. You remade me, Lord, and I am a new creature in the likeness of your son, so I'm asking you this day to help me glorify you, heavenly Father.*

He watched the fillies and colts romping in the meadow. They were totally free and unencumbered. They would be leaving before long, going to their new homes. He had tried his best to make sure each of them would have kind trainers. Robby had done his research on when to wean the foals from the mares and decided that three months, if they were halter trained, was the right time. Their new masters would be getting a wonderful Christmas present! They were all beautiful creatures that God had marked in unique ways. He thought about Robby mentioning that Alan and Clay were partial to Victory. One day that horse would make history. He hoped that Cole would get to see him soon. He missed Cole and Dana profoundly and could hardly wait for Thanksgiving when both would be home.

---

There was no response to Robby's knock at the front door of Al's home, so Robby took the liberty of opening the door, as Al was expecting him and Clay and Alan.

"Hello! Anyone home?"

He walked through the house and opened the door to the rear gardens, and again called out, "Al, are you here?"

"Hey, Robby, I'm in the rose garden. Give me a moment. I'll be right in."

Al came through the house and found the guys enjoying their fellowship in the living room. He thought to himself, *What a handsome group of young men!*

Robby stood up and greeted Al and made introductions.

"You guys have come a long way to consider purchasing one of our colts. How did you come across information on Ebony Mist and our new ranching operation?"

Clay took the lead. "We saw an article in a magazine written by Dana Fulton, and she seemed to have her facts straight on how to purchase the right stallion, not only for breeding purposes but for racing. When we saw the bloodline of The Mist, we knew this could advance our ranching endeavors."

Alan said, "We knew this was a long shot, traveling to England, making a purchase, and then arranging for the colt to be transported back to America, but we've taken risks in our business that others advised against, and profits have been turned, and our investments have given nice returns."

"So it is just the two of you in business?"

"Correct," Alan said.

Clay took a deep breath. "Mr. Statham, I have to be honest with you. I have followed you through the media since you stepped forward and saved my mom's life in St. Louis. I remember that court hearing as though it were yesterday. You placed your life on the line for my mom, and I can never thank you enough. When I saw the magazine article about your new venture, I not only wanted to see your business here, I wanted to meet you and thank you personally."

"You owe me no thanks, Clay. I did what I had to do. I had lived daily with thoughts about what happened to you after seeing newspaper articles about your kidnapping."

"Mr. Statham, my poor mom got caught up in trying to help a little boy; she did not set out to kidnap me. She witnessed only one side of the coin, and that was the neglect of my biological mother. When one goes back to the beginning, it is a sad story, but when one looks at how our great God worked everything out for His glory and reunited families, it is nothing short of a miracle! In His timing, He brought my biological family into my life, and of course that's when I met Alan. I have a wonderful relationship with my adoptive dad and my biological one as well. It would have been impossible for Alan and me to have such a successful business without the knowledge of Les Samuels, my adoptive father. He has been a successful rancher most of his life, and my adoptive mom has always embraced him in whatever risks he took. I also have a wonderful relationship with my biological father. After hearing the testimonies of Robby, Conner, and Mitch, I am confident it was meant for us to meet you."

Al said, "God has taught me that it doesn't matter what poor choices we've made in life; He is willing and able to turn any tragedy into triumph. When I was young, reckless, and wayward, I did not have the strength or willpower to free myself from bondage. But in God's divine grace and mercy, I went from being lost to found, from homeless to owning a home and having a family, from being bound by drugs to being set free by Jesus. God's mercy continues to astound me. We must always go forward. After all, we're called to be light bearers, not burden bearers."

Al and Clay shared much of their past, and Robby and Alan were riveted to their seats, speechless. There were tears shed, praises given to God, and a bonding of all four men. Around one o'clock, Rani came through the front door and suggested she prepare a light lunch for everyone. Naturally, there was a round of applause!

Al got up from his seat. "I have an idea. While Rani is getting refreshments prepared, let's go down to the stables and have a look at the foals."

"I was hoping you would suggest that," Alan said.

They walked through the house and out through the gardens to the stable.

Clay said, "I have never seen such beautiful roses."

"Rani's green thumb. She's the expert," Al said.

"I have never seen such talent in one little woman!"

"We would be lost without her. God has given her so much love, compassion, and gifts too numerous to mention. Plain and simply, our family could not do without her."

Robby's voice was full of excitement. "Hey, guys, look at Victory run. He is just like his dad! Already you can see he is a natural racehorse. He has such a long stride for being so young. I am amazed by this colt."

"My son, Cole, and Robby have taught me to love being a rancher. I could never go back to the corporate office atmosphere. Just watching this little colt run with such abandon gives me life!"

Clay said, "I totally agree, Mr. Statham."

"I understand from Robby that you have your eye on Victory."

"We do, but we also want to honor your wishes, and we know that you desire to keep him."

"I think he will one day make history. That cross on his head speaks volumes to me. What I desire is that Victory's life will give encouragement and hope to those who need it. Victory is my gift to you boys, and I hope through our meeting, you guys will always remember to pay it forward and give others second chances."

Clay said, "Mr. Statham, your gift is more than we could accept. We are most beholden to you, but this colt could easily be sold for $50,000 right now. We would be happy to purchase Spirit from you."

"No, boys, Spirit is not for sale. I shall keep him. Victory is yours but only as a gift."

Robby said, "There is no way out of this, guys. When Mr. Statham makes up his mind, that's that! He has been this way as long as I have known him."

Alan said, "We are speechless, Mr. Statham."

"Robby, you need to help Clay and Alan work out the details in arranging for Victory to get to the States in a month or six weeks when we separate him from the mare. I will commit to letting you safely escort the colt to the States, provided you will not be gone more than three to four days. You are another person we cannot do without around here!"

"Mr. Statham, you must know all of this is very difficult for us to process. We have never met anyone like you. We humbly accept your most generous gift and shall keep you abreast of Victory's progress. We would also be honored to have you visit our ranch whenever you come to the States," Clay said.

"Boys, I believe it has been God's will for us to connect. I needed to hear many of the things Clay related about his life. It has given me a sense of freedom when I think about my past. God desires that we operate in His freedom, and a great part of that is knowing that God can turn any mess we make into a message that can encourage or bring life to others. I am so happy both of you came our way. Remember to stay in touch, and we hope you'll visit one day again."

# Chapter 16

## *Ponderings and Reflections*

### Cole:

I shall be going home for the entire summer in just one short week! It seems too good to be true! This has been a great year, and even though I have missed Nya profoundly, the year has flown by. Professor Gordon and Graham could not have been more supportive of me. I am relieved to know Graham now has a great job that he loves and has asked Zina to marry him. Those two are perfect together. Oh my, there are two more who are perfect together, too! Dad and Dana deserve each other, and staying with them during the Christmas holidays was all the confirmation I needed to know without a doubt that God brought the two of them together. I find it interesting that I've had no dreams or visions since Zina's healing.

*Dear Lord, thank you for the many months of letting me truly rest in your peace. My days have been productive in class and on the debate team as well, and at night, you sang over me and gave me complete rest. Thank you, Father.*

### Nya:

I am ready to see my family in Leeds. They have all been so gracious to call and write letters, and I know when I see them, it shall be as if we were never apart! It is time for Dad and India to have their lives back as newlyweds. The three of us have enjoyed this gorgeous paradise and discovered many out of the way places to ride horses and experience nature as never before. I shall always want to come back and visit New Zealand, and I can hardly wait to show Cole this little piece of heaven on earth.

I thoroughly enjoyed reading Cole's journal that he sent me last month. Just reading through his heartfelt expressions this past year has made me realize the two of us are as connected as we've always been.

I'm so proud of Robby and his new ranching endeavors with Al, and I was more than pleased to hear that Ebony Mist won the Kentucky Derby race. Robby finally has a mission and a purpose. Can't wait to see him and spend time learning about his training techniques with The Mist!

*Dear Father, you've been so faithful to guide me and comfort me during the time I've spent away from Cole. I am grateful that both of us have been able to enjoy a full and rich life without one another and solely depend on you. Not sure how Cole feels in this particular passage, but, Father, I am ready to be married to the man you chose for me. Please guide us both by your Holy Spirit, in the sweet Name of Jesus.*

## Al:

Can hardly wait to see my boy, my son. He is a man now, and one with wisdom beyond what I can comprehend. It will be good to see Cole and Nya reconnected. Surprises await them, and I pray they will be pleased, for I have taken great liberties on their behalf. Building a place for their future has given me much pleasure, and like all projects, it was a team effort. Robby graciously gave us rights to part of his property for an entrance to the new house. The setting is complete with woods, creeks, and our meadow. When I think about the big house, ranch house, and now Cole's house, I cannot help but think about the three in a spiritual sense, Father, Son, and Holy Spirit. Dana worked long and hard on every detail of the interior of Cole and Nya's home. One would have thought she was designing it for herself, for she poured every ounce of her energy into the project to complete it in four months, as did the contractors and landscapers. If ever there was a dream house, this was it.

*Oh, Lord, you have given me the perfect wife. She thinks not of herself but places others first. She has brought passion into my very being. I am thankful for my wife, my son, Nya, Rani, Robby, Conner, Vera, little Austin, and all of our many friends in our church. You have bathed me with love, compassion, and joy. I praise your holy name, dear Lord, and desire to be your humble servant.*

### Rani:

What a whirlwind year! So many details, so much activity, but most of all a blessed journey with Al and Dana. Both have treated me like their mother. I can sense that Dana has tried to lessen my duties. I think she senses that I do not have the stamina I used to have. How she has had the energy and time to design and decorate Cole's house, plus help me with guests at the ranch house, is nothing short of a miracle! Everything for her seems effortless. She glows and laughs when she rolls up her sleeves! Never seen anyone with such a great attitude.

*Father, how you transform your children. Please bring our loved ones, Cole and Nya, safely home to us. Al is like a little boy waiting for Christmas. Please, Lord, let this be our happiest occasion yet when we are reunited this summer.*

## Summer's Lullaby

Nya arrived several days before Cole. Robby picked her up at the airport and talked nonstop all the way home.

"I've never seen you so exuberant, Robby. What's up?"

"Well, you've been gone for almost a year, and so much has happened that I don't know where to start or when to stop!"

"Let's start with your life, Robby."

"My life could not be any better. Mitch, the new jockey, and I have had quite a ride since you left. Ebony Mist's Derby win has brought so much interest and business to our ranch that we actually need more help."

"I can help now that I'm home. I would love to be a lady rancher!"

"This is a surprise to me. How about school, Nya? Don't you want to finish?"

"I can do most of my courses online now. Plus, all those little details will fall into place. I want to ride Ebony. I saw pictures of him in the paper, and he is truly a magnificent creature!"

"He is a unique horse and so fast. And there is another little horse who will be fast like his dad, and that is Spirit. If I were a betting man, I would say when Spirit is two, he will be bigger than his dad."

"Is he as striking as Ebony?"

"In a different way. He is more muscular and more powerfully built. Can't wait for you to see what awaits you!"

"Wow, what else awaits me? You are acting like there is some sort of surprise. You have a constant grin, Robby!"

"You'll have to wait, but yes, you shall be surprised!"

Rani was waiting at the front entrance with open arms. "Oh, Nya, how we've missed you!"

"Rani, I can hardly believe it! I'm home, finally."

Al picked her up and swung her around until both were dizzy.

Dana grabbed her and gave her a long, tight hug and said, "Welcome home, Nya."

"My precious family, so happy to be back. I shall never be gone this long from my home again—never!"

Rani slipped her arm around Nya and said, "Guess who prepared dinner for you this evening?"

"You, of course."

"Not me. Dana insisted that she prepare a meal for our princess."

"Dana, you are full of endless surprises, and I must say you are radiant, more beautiful than I remembered."

"Thank you, sweet Nya. Oh, yes, Robby, you must stay and join us for dinner. This is a celebration!"

"I accept. I'm going to take Nya's luggage upstairs first; be back in a moment."

Dana had set the table with their finest china and placed candles in the center of the table from end to end. The crystal reflected the light from the candles, and the aroma of duck and mandarin sauce was the perfect touch to stimulate everyone's appetites. A single rose was placed in front of each plate, and every rose was a different color. The blended fragrances created a magical atmosphere.

Dana stood smiling beside Al at the head of the table until Robby joined them.

Al said, "Take your seat, love, and let's say grace."

Nya said, "May I say the blessing, Al?"

"But of course."

"Our Father in heaven, how thankful our hearts are that you have brought us together once again. You tell us in your Word that you search the earth for hearts that are set apart for you, so you can shower your blessings. You indeed have showered all of us with your unfailing love, your goodness, your mercy, and your bounty. We are blessed to have Dana in our family. Only your divine design could have joined her to us. Father, bless her hands for preparing our meal, bless the families represented here tonight, bless this food to our bodies, and keep Cole safe when he travels home from Oxford. We honor you, and we delight in being filled with your Holy Spirit. It is with joyful hearts we bless you and give you praise tonight. Amen."

Rani had tears streaming down her cheeks. *My Lord and Savior, what a beautiful family you gave to me. How I have loved every minute with each and all of them since the first day Al Statham set foot on this property. I knew, Father, that he and his son were very special, perhaps earthly angels. My heart has been joyful since that first day of our meeting, and I've witnessed blessings on top of blessings and miracles on top of miracles. I have seen your hand working daily in the lives of Al and Cole to promote others. They live to do your bidding for others. And I think I may know a little secret because the Holy Spirit whispered to me ever so sweetly a few weeks back when Dana knelt down to smell and touch one of our new roses. She handled its velvet petals with such tenderness that I almost cried, and suddenly I knew that she was going to have a little one. Oh, Father, I'm sure she knows and is waiting for the right time to share with us all. My heart melts when I think about the joy this will bring Al, especially since he lost his daughter. Oh that this would be a little girl! Father, thank you for all you've let me be a part of, and all that*

*I've witnessed that has revealed Your Glory! You are an awesome God and constantly at work in your children's lives.*

———— ∿∾◦❍⦾🆁⦾❍◦∾∿ ————

As Nya watched the clouds swiftly move across the moon as she was falling asleep that night, hot tears spilled onto her pillow. Her joy was overflowing, and yet her heart hurt because Cole had not yet arrived.

*Oh Father, bring him home soon and let our union be one that we never have to part again. I've been brave, but now I feel more vulnerable and needy than ever. Perhaps it could have something to do with seeing Al and Dana together. I can see they are one flesh joined with you. This home could be summed up with two words, love and harmony. I want a home with Cole, dear Lord. I know life is never simple, but when we live in the moment led of your Holy Spirit, life can be joyful and lovely, for you, oh Lord, raise us above our circumstances. Your promises are true and keep us on solid ground. I love you, dear Jesus, and adore your Holy Spirit. Night, my precious Lord.*

———— ∿∾◦❍⦾🆁⦾❍◦∾∿ ————

Only a few more miles, and he would see his family. God had given him total clarity on all of his exams, and he knew that his marks would be high for the entire semester. His debate team had also done well. This had been a banner year for him at Oxford! And now he could forget his studies, relax, and enjoy the summer with family and friends.

He thought about his dream. Last night was the first time he remembered a dream in many months, actually since Zina's healing. But this dream was vague, and he remembered only the last part of it. A very young angel appeared to him in his dream, and she looked exactly like Molly. She was smiling and so very beautiful. He never let himself think about his mom or his little sister. The moment his mind wandered, he would immediately think upon something else. But today, for some reason, he let the thought of Molly tear his heart open to his deepest wound. Just maybe his dream was significant. Perhaps God was letting Molly bring the good news that Dad and Dana would have a child. Of course, that was it! *I'm going to have a little sister!* He knew beyond a doubt this was true.

*Father, you are so faithful to speak to me of things I do not know. You tell us in Jeremiah that you'll reveal great and wonderful things that we do not know; how I love that scripture! You have let me witness so many miracles, Lord Jesus, and I want only to continue to surrender my life to you and your perfect will. Please guide my every step, action, and reaction so my life may be pleasing to you, my Lord. How I love you, Lord Jesus.*

As he passed through the gate, he sounded his horn. Nya flew to the front entrance to greet him. She flung herself into his arms as soon as he stepped out of the car.

"Oh, Cole, surely heaven could not be better than this!"

They embraced for what seemed a lifetime. Cole held her at arm's length and soaked in her beauty, for she was an extraordinarily stunning woman. A year ago, a girl, the love of his life, left, and now a woman had returned. He instinctively knew he could never let her go. His heart was sold out to this woman. He knew Nya was God's choice for him. She was to be his wife!

"Nya, come close again, sweetheart. Let me hold you forever. Your hair, your skin, your breath, your spirit...yes, your spirit speaks of hidden treasures from above. To touch you is to know there is a God above who loves us!"

"Oh, Cole, I believe my heart will burst with desire and love for you. Let us never, never part again. I beg of you, Cole."

"No need to beg, Nya. I do not ever intend for us to be a part again, Lord willing."

"Cole, look across the meadow. Do you see the new addition?" "Yes, I guess it is Dad and Dana's dream home."

"You are right about it being a dream home but not your dad's. Cole, he built it for us!"

Cole was speechless.

"What are you thinking, Cole?"

"Let's walk over to the grass; this concrete is a little hard."

On bended knee, Cole brought Nya's hand to his lips and tenderly looked up into her eyes. "Will you marry me, Nya?"

"Yes, yes, yes!"

The two embraced until Al and Rani came on the scene. "Son, it is so good to have you home!"

"Been a long time since we made reference to a group hug—right, Dad?"

"Yes, Cole, but that's exactly what we need, son."

Al and Cole were both struggling to hold back the tears.

"Hey, Dad, where is Dana?"

"She is napping right now. I think she has overdone it lately, and I insisted she lie down for a couple of hours."

"We need to take good care of Dana and my little sister!"

"So God revealed to you that we are expecting a child?"

"Yes, Dad, and a little girl!"

Nya said, "When is our little angel due?"

"October, same time the mares will have their fowls. One celebration after another!

"Dad, Nya and I have another surprise. We are going to be married!"

"Son, surely you must know that is no surprise to any of us."

"Right, well, of course. Perhaps it was a surprise to me. You know I can be a bit slow at times! And just how did you get a house built in four months?"

"Team work, lots of hours, lots of hard work, and motivated by love!"

"I can't wait to see it, but first I want to see Dana and our little one who is being made in God's perfect image!"

Cole grabbed Rani, kissed her on the cheek, and said, "You are going to have another grandchild! What do you think about that?"

"I am thrilled and thankful. Right now I am grateful to God for safely bringing you home. All is right with my world."

———❧———

Upon awakening, Cole went down to Nya's room.

She felt a warmth above her face. "Cole, what is it? Are you okay?"

"Yes, just perfect. The sun will be rising soon, and I thought you would want to go to the stables, saddle up, and ride over to our home and check it out!"

"Sure, give me a minute to dress, and I'll come downstairs in about five."

Both were excited to see their precious Mystery and Samson. Mystery was pawing on the door of her stall. She instinctively knew Cole was home. These horses were like family to Cole and Nya.

"Mystery looks great, Cole. I don't think she lost weight this year as she did last."

"Dana and Dad have given all of the horses special attention since we've been away. I'm so thankful my dad enjoys riding as we do. It gives him a connection with purpose since he has retired."

"Cole, do you think we will always live here on the property?"

"That would be hard to say, for I do not know the mind of God and what He has purposed for us to do. But I do know deep within my spirit that you and I shall always be one with God."

"I have that same confidence."

"Okay, are you ready to see our home?"

"Let's go!"

In less than five months, a magnificent mini castle had been designed and constructed. The corbelled turrets on each side were dwarfs of the central tower and turret. Angelo had chosen exterior appointments with a Scots Baronial flair.

The front entrance to the castle was grand. The driveway divided into two lanes halfway to the house, and in the center were three beautiful fountains framed by rose gardens of only red roses. The brick had been painted white, and the double glass door entrance was framed in black marble. The roof was a charcoal slate tile, which was a handsome touch in contrast to the white exterior. There was a small glass elevator in addition to two staircases of mahogany wood. The lower level had two sitting rooms, a living room, library, kitchen, and two bathrooms. All of the lower level had vaulted ceilings with beautiful angles and lighting. The second level had the master suite, a library, sunroom, and an inside garden with an aquarium, plus an elaborate nursery. The third level had four bedrooms with adjoining baths, and a large game room with a mini kitchen. Neither Nya nor Cole could believe that this home had been built and grounds landscaped in less than five months. What a project for Angelo and his crew. Plus, Dana had to be exhausted from all the decisions regarding the interior. It was incredible. The stables in back were framed by the woods and a huge arena. The driveway itself was quite a feat, for it began on the back part of the wooded property and stretched down the side of the property and then wound around to the front before it split into two lanes.

Nya and Cole looked at each other shaking their heads. "How does your dad do it?"

"He reaches across human boundaries and thrives in God's confidence, knowing that what is not humanly possible is always possible with God. As long as I have known him, he has had that easygoing way that enables him to enjoy the journey. My dad has taught me so much."

"And me as well."

"Do you want to ride back into the woods where we first met?"

"Yes, I do. I shall never forget that day. We were only strangers for a moment before instantly being connected. I knew that very day I had met someone I would forever adore."

"And I knew that I had met the person that I could share the depths of my heart with, without any reservations."

"Cole, no matter where we find ourselves geographically, I believe we shall always return to our little castle and one day retire here. All of the property and homes are laced together with rich memories, and I am looking forward to making many more!"

"Tell me, are you ready to set the date for our marriage?"

"Yes, how about a July 4th wedding?"

"Sounds good to me, and perhaps Graham and Zina can join us since it's a holiday!"

"Cole, can we keep it simple so Rani and Dana will not work themselves into some kind of frenzy?"

"I was thinking along those same lines. How about immediate family and close friends—and have the ceremony at our church?"

"I like your plan!"

"There is the matter of a ring, and I have been thinking about this since I asked you to marry me. I would love to give you my mother's ring that Dad bought for her after his business became profitable. It is a princess-cut diamond encased in emeralds. It was designed especially for Mom, and I know she would be so proud to have you wear it. It would mean so much to me, too."

"Oh, Cole, I would be honored to wear your mom's ring. You are such a thoughtful man. I think that is one of the things I admire most about you. I would imagine it is because you are prayerful before you voice your opinion."

"Reliance upon the Holy Spirit is far superior to any thought I might have!"

"I agree."

"My stomach is talking to me. Let's race back to the stables and check out the breakfast menu. It will be interesting to see what the joint efforts of Rani and Dana bring to the table!"

The horses had not raced with the wind in a while, and both rebelled against tight reins. Mystery loved having her way when Cole was riding her. She won the race by several yards. Both horses were winded when they reached the stables.

"There is nothing like a full run across our meadow! Does life get any better?"

After they dismounted, Cole took Nya in his arms and kissed her forehead, her eyes, and her full lips.

"You know you'll be going to Oxford with me after all, don't you?"

"I realize that. Guess I should have conceded two years ago, right?"

"No, you needed your independence. You needed to explore in your own way. I'm glad to know you are reconnected with your family. And too, we both had some growing up to do!"

"Thanks to your dad, we'll have a month of bliss in our new home here before going back to Oxford. I'm looking forward to learning more about the ranching business from Robby, too."

"Nya, we'll learn together, pray together, and stay focused on being a blessing to others. As long as we place God first in our lives, He will tell us great and wonderful things we do not know."

"Cole, when I think upon our future, the hymn *When I Survey the Wondrous Cross* comes to mind ... 'When I survey the wondrous cross on which the Prince of Glory died, my richest gain I count but loss and pour contempt on all my pride.' May we both be cloaked with humility and live to serve our Master and Lord."

"One of my favorite verses in the Bible is Psalm 85:10, 'Love and faithfulness meet together; righteousness and peace kiss each other.' Oh that we would express our gratitude each and every day for His infinite mercy and grace that He has bestowed upon us through Christ, for He is our breath, our soul, our all."

———— ᨑᨕᨑᨑᨑ ————

July 2nd, two days before the wedding, a silver truck pulling a horse trailer appeared in the driveway. Al spotted it from the living room window and opened the front door. With the ranching business booming, he never knew when to expect the unexpected. Ebony Mist had become quite the celebrity!

Al recognized the young man immediately when he stepped out of the truck.

"Graham, welcome. We are so happy that you were able to come celebrate with us. And this must by your wife, Zina."

"Yes, Mr. Statham, let me present my lovely bride."

"Zina, we have heard so many wonderful things about you and indeed are grateful you and Graham could come to the wedding!"

"I guess it looks as though we brought our own horses to ride, but in all actuality, we are looking forward to riding some of your horses! The horse we brought is an American Saddlebred mare. She is our gift to Cole and Nya, and she has recently been bred, so we come bearing two gifts!"

"How generous of you, Zina. I'm sure this will be quite a surprise for Cole and Nya."

"Mr. Statham, our gift of Autumn Spirit is my way of saying thank you to Cole for saving my life. Our Lord used Cole to give me my life back, and I could really never repay him, but when we rode together all those weeks last year during my healing, he admired the gaits of Autumn and wanted to incorporate her breed into your ranching business. Autumn has been a perfect little mare, and I know she will be an asset and a pleasure for all of you to ride."

"Well, let's bring her out. I can't wait to see her!"

As Zina was leading Autumn out of the trailer, Cole joined them.

"Zina, Graham, what a wonderful surprise that you came early. We can all ride together! I see you brought your own mount and my favorite of all your horses."

Zina handed the reins to Cole. "She is now yours. Our gift of thanks to you."

"I don't know what to say."

Al said, "I believe 'thank you' might be appropriate."

"But, Zina, this is your favorite little mare. You said so yourself."

"We give others our best gifts, and I seem to remember this is what you taught me."

"I am overwhelmed and most appreciative. Your thoughtfulness and generosity overwhelm us. Nya will be so delighted over Autumn! Let's take her to our stables and introduce her to Mystery, Samson, and Rapha. I know our horses will graciously accept Autumn. After we get her settled in, we'll drive over to the new home Dad built for us, and we'll get you two settled in and give you a little time to rest and relax before we all saddle up and ride this afternoon."

"Cole, is that your home across the meadow?"

"It is, and I know you will be comfortable having your own space. After all, you are newlyweds ... perhaps a second honeymoon, right?"

Zina laughed. "I was thinking that same thing!"

---

The day of celebration had arrived. The stage was set, and the hearts of Cole and Nya were bursting with joy and love.

"Rani, have we forgotten anything?"

"If we have, it will go unnoticed because you look perfect!"

Rani had helped Nya make her wedding dress. Al had ordered the material from a famed fabric shop in Paris. He had also ordered pearls from the same jewelry maker who designed Nya's wedding ring, which of course was Cole's mother's ring. The pearls were small with tiny holes through the center so they could be hand-stitched carefully to the neckline of the wedding dress and the veil.

The pearls were white, pink, and pale blue. Dana, Nya, and Rani had labored late into the nights placing all the finishing touches on the dress.

She looked at herself carefully in the full-length mirror. More than anything she wanted to be the pure bride that Cole deserved and God would honor. She was pleased with the simple yet elegant design of the dress. Her hair was lifted up and pulled back on the sides with the back flowing naturally under the long veil.

Rani thought she was the most beautiful bride she had ever seen. Her dark hair under the veil brought out the blue in her enormous gray eyes. The tiny pink pearls brought a slight pale pink glow to Nya's complexion, and she looked like an angel. Tears fell from Rani's checks. What a union this would be today.

Cole and Al were leaving for the church. Conner was to bring Nya, Rani, and Dana.

Cole looked more handsome than Al had ever witnessed. He looked like a man. Al thought, *Where did my little boy go? How did the years pass so quickly? Oh, son, your mother would be so proud of the man you've become. Seems like yesterday you, Molly, and your mom were giving me a group hug ... only yesterday. Oh, heart of mine, let's move forward, for this is the day the Lord hath made, and we shall rejoice and be glad in it.*

"Dad, hey, where are your thoughts? You look miles away."

"Just took a detour down memory lane, son, but I'm back!"

"It is time we departed, Dad. I know this is a new journey for us all, especially Nya and me, so let me say in these moments before change forever takes place, I love you and appreciate all you've taught me about life, love, and our great God. One day I hope to impart wisdom to my children like you've always extended to me. It has never been what you thought but how the Holy Spirit led you to think, speak, and treat others. Guess what I'm saying is you are a hard act to follow, Dad!"

"I could not be more proud to call you my son. You are a beautiful man inside and out, and I know God will use you in a mighty way to bring glory unto Himself. I love you, Cole."

"Dad, I love you, too."

———⁓⌇⌇⌇⌇⌇⌇⌇⌇⌇⌇⌇———

Cole and the pastor stood at the altar. Roses and candles framed the front of the chapel, and there were no more than forty family members and friends attending. The afternoon sun reflected colors of the rainbow as it shone through the stained-glass windows.

As Nya stood in back of the chapel with her dad on her right side and Al on her left, Cole walked over to the piano and picked up the microphone. The pianist played the introduction, and Cole sang "Our Father Who Art in Heaven." His beautiful tenor voice left no eye dry. He sang from the depth of his soul to his awesome God, and it was apparent to everyone how very much he loved God.

As Nya was escorted to the front of the chapel by Al and Evan, Cole had never seen such a glorious sight. What a gift God was giving him. A wife to have and to hold for as long as he would live. He would hold her loosely, for she belonged to God. She was the most beautiful woman he had ever looked upon. *Oh Father in heaven, please sanction this union. Help me to be the man that Nya will always respect and trust, and help me to tenderly care for her and any children born into this marriage. I am placing both of us in your hands, Father.*

Cole and Nya knelt together, and Pastor Elliott prayed over them.

"Today, Cole and Nya have expressed a desire to share their personal vows with one another in the presence of God and this congregation. Nya, will you please say what is on your heart."

> *"My dearest Cole, I gave you my heart years back, but on this day I commit to letting you keep my heart forever. After our awesome God, you shall always be first in my life. As is the church in her relationship to Christ, I shall be to you, my love. No matter what our future holds, I promise to stand by your side and be your obedient and faithful wife and love you as long as God gives me breath. May our heavenly Father join us as one forevermore."*

She brought his hands to her lips and kissed them both.

Pastor Elliott continued, "Now, Cole, you may share your vows."

> *"My dearest Nya, our love was ordained and sustained by God above. He gave me eyes for only you when I was thirteen years old, and I thank Him for keeping both of us pure for one another until this day that He appointed. Our gracious God will lead us both to be vessels for His service in accordance with His plan. He will carry us through the present as well*

*as the uncertainties of the future. I promise to be faithful to you as long as we both shall live, and love and protect you as Christ does His church. I give you my hand and my heart as a sanctuary of warmth and peace, and pledge my love, devotion, faith, and honor as I join my life to yours."*

"Cole and Nya have given themselves to each other by solemn vows, with the joining of hands and the giving and receiving of rings. I pronounce that they are husband and wife in the Name of the Father, and of the Son, and of the Holy Spirit. Cole, you may kiss your bride."

The reception held at the church was special and joyful, and everyone paid tribute to the bride and groom. Afterward, all guests departed, including Graham and Zina, who said their goodbyes at the church and left for Oxford with full and happy hearts for their dear friends—friends who would journey together with them for a lifetime.

Cole and Nya would spend their honeymoon night in their new home in their very own bedroom. Rani and Dana had made sure that every detail was covered. Roses, candlelight, refreshments, and of course leaving the exterior lights on to light their path. The little castle would finally have its king and queen!

———

At the first light of day, Cole stirred and pulled Nya close. From the bedroom window, he could see the horses had been let out of the stables and were frolicking in the meadow. A new day and a new life.

*Father, how utterly faithful you are to me. Thank you for my dream last night of two children, a little girl and a little boy running and playing in front of our home here, and both the same age! I praise you for the lives of the twins you have placed in the womb of my beautiful and worthy wife. With everything that is within me, I place both of these children in your hands; I give them back to you and ask that by your Holy Spirit, you guide me each and every day in loving them, bestowing your wisdom and teaching them your ways. Lord and Master, my wife and I honor and bless you this glorious day. Amen.*

This novel was inspired by the Holy Spirit
and written for the glory of God!

—J. Laura Chandler, 04/07/17

Printed in the United States
By Bookmasters